DEMON WALKING

Dragon Point Six

EVE LANGLAIS

Copyright © October 2017, Eve Langlais

Cover Art by Yocla Designs © June 2017

Produced in Canada

Published by Eve Langlais

http://www.EveLanglais.com

eBook-ISBN: 978 1988 328 980

Print-ISBN: 978 1988 328 99 7

Prologue

W hat a lovely day to get rid of a body.

The countryside proved lush, the foliage the bright green of spring, the breeze carrying a hint of the summer warmth to come. One could almost ignore the smell of decay, the kind that reeked of meat left out too long.

His fault. He'd been delayed. Now, he paid for it, the rancid smell wafting free from the bedspread he'd wrapped the corpse in. The quicker he buried the body, the better. He just had to find a fresh spot. Harder than it sounded since he'd already entombed a few.

Humans were plentiful in these parts, although they did make noisy meals unless properly subdued.

He should also make mention that humans didn't make for the tastiest of treats, but they did curb his gnawing hunger. Only for a short while, though. What he really craved? The delicacy that made him salivate? Dragon.

One full-grown dragon could sustain him for much

longer than a few days. It tickled his taste buds and left him feeling satisfied and euphoric. Alas, they were hard to find, not to mention that he couldn't eat too many at once or the dragons would notice and take offense. Spoilsports.

Knowing they'd crucify him if they caught on meant he had to be careful about his meals. Getting discovered at this point wouldn't do at all. He needed to build his strength if he wanted to eventually rule this world. After all, he'd not escaped Hell to sink into obscurity.

On the contrary, now that he had a new lease on life, he had plans. Lofty goals for this new world that was ripe for the taking.

Another ripe thing? The body. Something wicked this way oozed.

His nose wrinkled. Time to bury it. He made quick work of the soil, creating a hole big enough to hide the body.

There was nothing to be done about the scar of dirt that showed against the lush greenery all around. Good thing no one inhabited this part of the land. Before long, the mark of his passing would be overgrown.

Task done, he closed his eyes and inhaled. A nice, deep breath. After the staleness of hell, the fresh air of earth proved so sweet.

Almost as sweet as the woman he met in a tavern a few days later when the hunger gnawed him again.

Petite and human, she batted her lashes as she clung to his arm, the fumes of the alcohol she'd imbibed emanating with every word.

Exiting the vehicle that he'd learned to drive— though not without mishap—she'd gaped with proper appreciation at the home he'd appropriated.

"Wow, what a big castle you have."

Not technically his, but the former owner couldn't exactly complain about his confiscation of it. It took only a few hours of intimidation and torture to convince the blubbering mess to give him access to anything he wanted. In return, he'd promised not to eat the owner of the castle. Once he had everything he needed, he'd kept his word and killed the man, but didn't take one bite.

Why ruin his palate with an old, balding man when he could dine on sweet, young flesh? Not to mention that he enjoyed throwing a bit of sex into the mix—another thing he'd missed while in that hellhole.

Nothing better than the feel of nails raking down his back, a soft, feminine voice urging him to go, "faster." The slap of flesh as he sank balls-deep, and then, in the moment of climax…he struck. Much like a vampire, he bit hard enough to break skin, and as the coppery blood spilled into his mouth, he called on his magic. Spoke the guttural enchantment that allowed him to take nourishment from the blood.

His siphoning of her life force started out pleasurable. She moaned as her body writhed. As the climax hit, the muscles of her sex clenched tightly. But as he sucked at her life essence, ingesting every last delicious drop, she began to panic. Shoved at him. Thrashed. They never seemed to grasp that by then, it was too late.

In her final moment, her mouth opened wide in a silent scream, and her eyes gazed at him in horror. Only then did he come.

"Fuck it's good to be alive," he yelled as he spurted hotly into her still twitching body.

Done, he rolled off the gray and already cooling woman. Her youth and beauty gone, along with her life.

He uttered a satisfied sigh before reaching for a cigarette, his hunger sated for a few more days.

There was another body to bury, but he didn't mind. He was free. Powerful. And best of all, alive.

Chapter One

"What a wonderful day to be alive!" Elspeth exclaimed as she twirled in the fresh air, arms spread wide.

Someone groaned. "You do realize it's gray and soggy."

"Nothing wrong with gray. My grandma has gray hair, and she's awesome!" She was also quick with the wooden spoon, which led to Elspeth being light on her feet.

Babette peered one-eyed, much like a pirate, at the overcast, dripping sky. "I spent an hour straightening my hair, and now because you insisted on having that cab drop us a mile from the house, it's ruined."

"Exercise does the body good."

"That's an infomercial slogan, and again, since you seem to not realize it, it's raining!" Babette shook her fist at the dark clouds.

"Isn't it glorious?" Elspeth held out her hands to feel the sprinkling raindrops, the moisture a balm to the skin. "I love the rain. It's nature's way of nourishing the soil, which, in turn, allows life to flourish and bloom. April showers bring May flowers," she sang.

"Gag me with a spoon."

"Why dirty a spoon when you can just shove your fingers down your throat? Do you need help? You can borrow mine. They're long." She did so love to offer aid to her friends. Not that Babette considered herself Elspeth's best friend yet. She was shy that way, claiming she didn't need one.

However, Elspeth knew better. Now that Deka had gone off with that handsome beau of hers, Babette needed someone to take her spot—and Elspeth was determined to be that girl! Especially since her last best friend ran away.

That was the last time she listened to her mother when she said "if you love something set it free." Her friend took flight and left Elspeth with an opening.

Babette slapped down Elspeth's hand. "I don't need your help to throw up. Just keep talking, that will do the trick."

"I'm a little concerned about your obsession with vomiting. I do hope this isn't a cry for help. Bulimia is a very severe illness."

"I am not bulimic."

"That's the spirit." But Elspeth made a note to keep a close eye on Babette just in case. Arranging an intervention was exactly the kind of thing a good friend did. In the meantime, someone needed to know she was loved just the way she was.

"Put me the fuck down!" squealed her almost-best friend.

At a touch over six feet, Elspeth knew how to give the best hugs, the kind that lifted a person off the ground and made them feel special. Ignoring the false protests, she squeezed Babette—who didn't even reach her chin—tightly.

Crack. Something in Babette's spine adjusted, and not for the first time, Elspeth wondered if perhaps her talents were wasted.

I should be a doctor!

She'd tried to apply at the local clinic. They'd declined, citing some need for an actual medical degree. Crazy talk. Who needed certification in chiropractic medicine when it came naturally via Elspeth's super-duper therapeutic hugs?

"Would you stop it already," Babette said, pretending to sound grumpy. Elspeth knew it was just a sham because, hello, everyone loved a hug. "We're gonna be late for the meeting with our king."

How responsible of her new best friend to remind her. "Late for a very important date! We can't have that. Fear not, my short-legged bestie. I'll get us there on time." Tossing Babette over her shoulder, Elspeth ran for the large house, a mansion by most standards, but to dragons, it was just a house—with a few dozen bedrooms and a ballroom fit for royalty. Human royalty, to be specific.

Dragons preferred to party in the open air when possible, where they could spread their wings and fly. There was nothing like feeling the air currents under a dragon's wings.

Elspeth had been doing a lot more flying lately now that the world—AKA the humans—knew of their existence. It had become hard to deny with social media having caught them several times now. The oft-repeated excuse of "fake news!" no longer worked. Especially after a dragon in France went on a talk show and demonstrated live for an audience. Was offered a book deal right after. Only, that dragon disappeared.

The Fleur de Lys Sept—which eschewed a color because they prided themselves on their diversity—claimed they'd placed the dragon in protective custody since the world knew her face.

How kind of them, especially since the North American Septs told their members that they'd be skinned alive if they pulled a stunt like that.

Elspeth had no interest in talking to the media; however, she didn't mind the world knowing about their existence.

Sure, some of her kind grumbled about knights coming out of the woodwork to slay them, and the internet ruminated about dragon hoards—and there seemed to be an inordinately high number of ladies claiming to be virgins on dating sites—but personally, Elspeth thought everyone was happy to discover their existence.

Why, just the other day, she'd made some children extra happy by taking them for a ride in the sky. Their mother, obviously upset that she was too heavy to join them, had screamed and sobbed on the ground the entire time.

When Elspeth landed and returned her brood, she'd patted the mother on the head and trilled, "You're welcome." The woman peed herself in excitement.

It felt good to give back to society.

Entering the house via a door that opened just in time—unlike the last time when she'd crashed into it—she remembered to kick off her shoes. Cleanliness was only part of the reason.

With Babette firmly situated on her shoulder, Elspeth dashed down the hall of the house, the marble floors—streaked with gold and polished to a high gleam —slippery. Once she'd gained enough speed, she slid, her momentum carrying her.

"Whee!" she squealed. Babette groaned. Probably because she was upset that she'd forgotten to wear socks and couldn't glide, too.

Elspeth really should keep some tucked on her person for the next time, so her bestie could join her in the fun.

She executed a turn to brake by the double doors leading into the king's office—formerly the Silver Sept's formal library. Rather than take over the Silvergrace matriarch's office, the king had opted for a grander space with books. Elspeth assumed the king had chosen it because he was so smart. However, others claimed it was because he liked the easy access to the garden, where he could escape.

Which was also really smart. Despite the fact that their Golden king had mated, some of the more eager mamas with marriageable daughters were still trying to change his mind.

Luckily for Elspeth, her mother had stopped trying to play matchmaker, especially after what had happened in Hawaii. Apparently, Akamu—her suitor—still wouldn't go anywhere near the ocean.

"Put me down," Babette demanded, giving a little wiggle.

Elspeth neatly flipped Babette onto her feet and exclaimed, "We're here. And on time. You're so very welcome."

Her bestie peered at her via a squinted eye. Did she need glasses? A monocle would be cooler.

"Don't you dare lay hands on me again," Babette grumbled.

Elspeth didn't take offense. Poor Babette did her best to hide how she suffered after Elspeth's gentle letdown where she'd explained to a gaping Babette that she preferred boys. But Elspeth had thought it better to tell Babette upfront than lead her on.

"Sorry for not taking into account your unrequited lust for me. It won't be long before you meet someone you can lavish your desires on."

"I desire to throttle you."

"Have you been exercising with those hand grips I gave you? I think we both remember how well it worked last time." Playful Babette had pounced on Elspeth and held on tightly to her throat, yelling, "Fall, damn you!"

Instead, Elspeth giggled and sent a wiggling Babette flying.

"One day, a piano will fall on your head, pushed out of a window, by me."

"Just like a cartoon!" Elspeth clapped her hands. "I can't wait." Another person who shouldn't wait? The king.

It wouldn't do to be late by standing around outside his office. Elspeth raised her fist and solidly rapped on the door. Taking a step back, she stood patiently in front of it, minding her manners.

"How are we supposed to surprise people in flagrante delicto if we give them warning we're coming in?"

Her bestie had so much to learn when it came to

caring about others and good manners. Good thing Elspeth didn't mind teaching her.

"It's rude to just enter."

"Says you. I say, out of my way." Babette shifted left, and Elspeth leaned to block. A quick dash right saw Babette bouncing off her arm.

Hands planted on her hips, Babette blew a hunk of hair out of her face and huffed, "Let me pass."

Elspeth shook her head. "We have to wait."

"Wait for what? We're expected."

"Manners, my dear friend. They're for everyone. Did you know, if everyone used their manners, crime would drop sixty-five percent per day?"

"What about the other thirty-five percent?"

"They're murdering psychopaths who weren't hugged enough as children." At least according to a blog Elspeth subscribed to. The narrator wasn't a true doctor or scientist or anyone with a degree for that matter. But he had started the online group dedicated to the use of hugs to prevent the apocalypse.

Someone shouted, "Come in."

"About time," muttered Babette.

As Elspeth politely opened and held the door for her bestie, Babette swept past, her petite frame wearing a pink velvet jumpsuit with *Hottie* printed across the butt.

Elspeth tended to wear more practical items, given she had a thirty-six-inch inseam. Custom-made slacks and denim comprised her daily wear for the most part. However, she did have a fetish for Rockabilly-style dresses in vivid colors with skirts that flared. And bright red lipstick.

Today, she wore a shade with a name that almost made her blush, but she loved it—Crimson Blowjob.

Mother would have a fit if she knew, whereas Elspeth got a thrill each time she rubbed her lips together.

Now if only she had a man in her life to apply that lipstick to. Alas, a tall woman was intimidating to a lot of men—even a dragon one. Most couldn't handle her zest for life.

But one day, my dragon prince will come. Yes, dragon, because the police said if she accidentally put one more guy in the hospital with broken bones, they'd investigate her for assault. As if she were to blame for their poor calcium intake growing up.

Now, if only she could find him. She'd seen his face in her dreams, but he'd proven elusive.

Babette didn't pay any mind to the office they entered. Probably because, much like in school, her bestie was used to being sent to the office, whereas Elspeth never got called in.

Everyone should be a teacher's pet. It came with so many perks. And it made her classmates so jealous. She could still hear their chanting—"*Brown nose. Ass kisser*"— as they tried to overcome their disappointment that they weren't the coveted student.

Given Elspeth rarely got called in front of important people, she looked around with curiosity at the large space. It truly was a library, the kind she loved, with towering bookcases that spanned a few levels and a ceiling that stretched high above. The shelves covered the entire width and height of the walls and were equipped with silver rails upon which hung wooden ladders.

Wouldn't it be fun if someone threw on some kind of lighthearted musical song and she had to scamper up those ladders then swing across, singing as she looked for books?

It had worked well for the princess in that movie, and in the end, she'd gotten the beast. Who'd proven more handsome when hairy than shaven.

Alas, the few knickknacks in the room didn't animate to form an orchestra, which meant that Elspeth could only stare longingly at the shelves, crammed with tomes of all kinds. Leather-bound and dusty, the silver leaf on the spines faint. The more recent books displayed the advances in printing technology with cardboard spines.

According to Babette, the shelf of romances no longer held a place of pride since the king wasn't a fan. He'd opted to replace them with rolled-up scrolls from ancient times.

A smart guy no matter what the others said. Nothing wrong with being a meticulous geek. Yet Elspeth knew of the grumblings. The treacherous words. "*When will he take us to war?*"

The dragon Septs didn't seem to realize that Remiel wanted peace, not battle. From all accounts, he shared some of Elspeth's philosophies—without the hugging.

Pity he was taken. Even whilst sitting behind his desk, he presented the image of the type of man who would attract a nubile dragoness.

Big and broad-shouldered, his short hair a pure gold tone, his eyes shone brightly as he perused them.

Having practiced for this moment, Elspeth dropped into a deep curtsy, miming holding a skirt despite her pants. "Oh, glorious king, I am so honored to have been called into your esteemed presence that I might serve you in any which way you need."

Babette, overcome with the regal presence of their

13

newly anointed king, made a retching sound. Poor thing. Her nerves must be bothering her again.

"Rise, um, Elsie, right?"

"If my king decrees it, then so shall it be." Elspeth beamed. Such an honor to already have a nickname with the king.

"And I see you brought Babette."

"Yo." Her almost-best friend saluted him with two fingers.

The king slammed shut the lid of his laptop. "Thank you for coming. Have a seat."

Choosing the left seat, Elspeth perched with her knees tightly pressed together, her back ramrod straight, and her hands demurely folded in her lap. Whereas Babette flopped onto the chair alongside her, one leg hanging over the armrest, and snapped a piece of gum before saying, "What's up, Remy?"

Shocked, Elspeth leaned over and whispered, "That's our king."

"And?" replied the woman who was blowing bubbles and then popping them with a loud crack.

"We should address him as 'your highness' or 'your majesty.'"

The king cleared his throat. "Um, that's not necessary. Remy is fine."

Elspeth almost fainted with the honor. The king had given her permission to address him by his first name—and a shortened version at that. This would go in her scrapbook as the bestest day ever, supplanting this morning's bestest moment when her mother had surprised her with bacon and a message to, "Get your ass to the big house. They need volunteers for a mission."

How exciting! Given it would be a great honor to

serve, of course she'd dragged Babette along. Although she'd had to fib a little, teeny-tiny bit to get her bestie to come, replacing the word *volunteer* with *chosen*.

"Why are we here? Elsie, over there,"—Babette jerked a thumb, quickly adopting the king's new name for her—"said you wanted to see me."

"I was looking for volunteers—"

"You mean this is optional?" Babette straightened. "Then I am out of here." Her best friend—because, obviously, only a BFF would call her by her new nickname—made to rise, only to stop as Remy—giggle—spoke.

"Yes, optional because I only want volunteers who aren't deterred by danger."

"Danger?" Babette plopped down and leaned forward. "Exactly what kind of danger?"

Did it matter? Elspeth clapped her hands. "We accept."

"Slow down, Elsie. We don't even know what he wants yet," Babette interjected. "Or how much it pays. We are being paid, right?"

The king gave a solemn nod. "Of course. A flat stipend per day plus expenses. A bonus if you save the realm from grave danger as per"—he shuffled some papers on his desk and held up a thick sheaf—"section nine A of the forty-fifth article on subjects participating in an investigative capacity for the crown."

Fancy mumbo-jumbo talk for getting paid to go on an adventure. The dragons hadn't survived this long without a proper king by chance. They had a charter of rights and rules—so many, many rules—that outlined all kinds of behavior.

Most Septs tended to pick and choose which they

followed; however, Remiel and his newly formed leadership had opted to use them as a baseline for drawing the Septs together for the greater good and protection of dragons.

"If we're getting paid, then I'm in," Babette declared before Elspeth could get over her excitement at the fact that she was going on another mission.

She'd thought it exciting when she got sent to the secret lair of the king's brother, Samael, and then got invited to fight in the great battle against the dragon mage, Voadicia. Front-line spot! Apparently, she'd acquitted herself well because here she was, about to embark on her second dangerous mission.

"Count me in, too!" Elspeth exclaimed.

The king blinked. Probably in pride at their willingness to serve the crown. "Aren't you going to wait to hear what the mission entails before accepting?"

"Considering I need a whole new wardrobe"—because poor Babette had lost her appetite and weight when she found out the woman she'd fallen in love with was actually a homicidal dragon mage from another dimension using her to get information and rule the world—"I'm sure it can't be that bad."

"And where my best friend goes, I go," Elspeth declared.

"We're not best friends," Babette growled.

"Yet," Elspeth sang. But in her heart, she knew. Best friends forever.

"While I only requested one volunteer, two is probably even better. Especially since I'm not sure what we're facing."

"Is that bitch Voadicia back, making trouble?" Babette asked. Which seemed unlikely, given she'd been swallowed by an alternate dimension. "I wouldn't mind tearing her into meat chunks and feeding her to an ogre."

"And I shall spread the excrement created to fertilize the fields."

Both Babette and Remiel stared at her. Elspeth clapped her hands as she had her opportunity to spread her message of *love my planet*.

"Reduce, reuse, recycle. It goes for everything. Bodies, too."

"In this case, there is no body," Remiel said. "As far as we know, she's still trapped in that alternate dimension. And according to my scientists, she won't be getting out of there alive."

"What if she sucks the souls of the creatures in that dimension and stays strong?" asked Babette.

"That's a problem about a thousand years away. I'll let the future kings deal with it. Our situation is less grave and happening right now, in Ireland. I'm not even sure if there is a problem. However, the Emerald Sept has asked me for help."

"Is it leprechauns?" Elspeth asked. The books she'd read indicated that they were foul-tempered little creatures that tasted sour, but Elspeth believed they were just misunderstood—and probably in need of some overnight marinating in a vanilla-sugar mix before roasting over a fire.

Not that she ate meat anymore. Elspeth was a vegetarian—going on two weeks now. She'd started as a vegan but couldn't live without cheese.

Now, she opted for meals that didn't bleed, but she would admit, it wasn't easy to ignore the delicious protein that kept taunting her. She'd dreamed of a cow last night, with great big eyes, asking why she'd forsaken his delicious rump roast.

"I don't think it's those pesky buggers," Remiel stated, interrupting her salivation over the thought of burgers charbroiled to perfection. "While no one has caught anything on camera, there are eyewitness reports of a flying creature and missing people."

"Is it a dragon?" Babette asked.

"Maybe. But it seems unlikely. According to the history books"—he swept a hand, indicating some shelves behind him—"there are only rare incidences where dragons have ingested people. Usually, the complaints are about missing livestock."

"If it's not a dragon, then what other flying creatures are we aware of that do eat humans?" Babette asked.

Elspeth raised her hand and wiggled on her chair.

The king looked her way. "You know what it is."

"Not exactly, but I do know of a few races that fit the bill. Griffons." Extremely rare. "Harpy." Which did not taste like chicken. "Giant vampire bat."

"Those aren't able to carry a person," Babette noted.

"Maybe they were small people."

"Maybe we shouldn't get sidetracked," said their wise king. "As of now, attempts to bait and corral the creature have failed."

"Bait how?" When Elspeth's mother wanted to find her, she baked cookies. No one could resist fresh-baked goodness.

"Having some hunters meander around the areas it's hit, looking like easy snacks."

"Hunters never look easy," Babette remarked, and Elspeth had to agree. When predators roamed, they held themselves a certain way. That attitude was what separated the hunter from the prey.

"Whatever it is, the few times the hunters have come close, they failed. It's as if they're chasing a shadow."

The term *shadow chasing* reminded Elspeth how she used to do that as a child. Then, one day, she managed to catch her shadow and hug it. It never appeared again. She liked to think it had gone on to a better place.

"Is that it then?" Babette asked. "Hunt down the mysterious thing in the sky? Seems like an easy enough case. Where's the danger?"

"Did you not hear the part where I mentioned people going missing?"

"And?"

Remy expanded. "As in gone, never to return."

"People disappear." Babette's shoulders rolled. "Happens all the time to the puny humans."

On account that they were low on the food chain. It was why Elspeth had started a group to have them recognized as valuable household pets. Thus far, she was the only member, and she'd yet to find a human that didn't run away. The next time she adopted a stray from the streets, she'd have to install a taller fence—and electrify it for their own safety.

"Actually, it's not just humans missing. A few dragons have disappeared, too."

"Cool," Babette exclaimed. "Real danger. I was beginning to think you were paying me to take a vacation."

Her enthusiasm was contagious. Elspeth smiled and clapped her hands. "Fear not, oh mighty leader. Your loyal subjects shall move with haste to the scene of the crime and ferret out the culprit, as well as rescue anyone we can find."

"After I go shopping." Babette held out her hand. "If you'll just give me your credit card."

Remy steepled his fingers. "This could be serious."

"We shall treat this mission with the utmost respect, Your Majesty. We shan't return until we've succeeded." Elspeth held her hand over her heart as she gave her solemn oath.

"We'll kick ass, no worries." Babette waggled her fingers.

Remy sighed as he handed over a credit card. "Be careful, would you? If I had anyone else to send, I would, but with our coming out to the general populace, we've found ourselves busier than usual. Some of the younger members of the Septs seem to think they can gallivant about with impunity. I've got the farmers' association calling me, claiming we're eating their livestock. Congress trying to pass a bill that would force us to lodge flight plans every time we go above a thousand feet. Then there are the fake websites popping up claiming to sell dragon parts."

"Mine's not fake," Babette exclaimed. "I'm selling legitimately used panties."

Remy stared at her. "Dare I ask why?"

Babette shrugged. "Beats washing them."

"Perhaps I should find someone else."

Elspeth jumped in. "Don't worry. We've got this. We promise to leave no rock unturned. No mountaintop unexplored."

"No tavern unvisited." Babette winked. "We got this, boss."

"That's what I'm afraid of."

"If we're done"—Babette rose from her chair— "we should get going before the stores close. I've got lots of shopping to do and panties to wear before we leave."

An ecstatic Elspeth was permitted to go along and carry said purchases. Babette even let her wear some of the panties she had to mail.

Her plan to become best friends was working!

Chapter Two

"That won't work. I can't be expected to visit the market and shop like a peasant." Luc—short for Lucifer—the last living branch of the Shining Ones, all dead save for him, paced in front of the cell holding the old man he'd captured. "Since when does a ruler have to purchase his own goods? Shouldn't the shopkeepers be bringing their wares to me?" And then donating them if they wished to stay in his good graces?

Luc might not have much experience with this world and its customs; however, he'd learned enough to know that the wealthy and powerful didn't do things like everyone else.

The old fellow, perched on a stool, sipping from a cup, shrugged. "Don't get snippy with me just because you don't like it. If you want to buy things, then you must go to the store."

"According to my mother, back in the day—"

The fellow interrupted. "Times have changed. You asked how to replenish the larder in the castle, and I told you. Don't blame me because you dislike the answer."

Luc's lips pursed. The old human had much temerity speaking to him thus. Yet, he'd asked for the truth. Or else...

"But what if I don't want to leave the castle and mingle with the humans?" Lowly creatures that lacked the ability to admire his greatness. Luc had gone amongst them a few times, enough to know he didn't enjoy their company one bit.

"Then don't leave the castle. Don't do anything. That's entirely your choice. Although, if you choose to skip shopping, then you'll get awfully hungry."

"There are other options for sustenance that don't require replenishing the larder." Luc eyed the man in the cell. "I could always eat you."

The fellow snorted. "Oh, please. We both know I'm old and stringy. Not even worth the trouble. Besides, if you eat me, then who will answer your questions?"

Good point. "I don't like your world." But it did beat living in his old one. A dimension his jailors had named Hell. It wasn't always a nightmare place. Once upon a time, it had practically been paradise.

According to his parents, the dragons who'd invaded centuries ago had killed his dimension. In their quest to live, the beasts had destroyed the lushness that used to imbue the land. Siphoned every ounce of life from it and then turned on its occupants. Luc was the only thing to survive.

And now he'd have his revenge.

"You sound like a petulant child." Alfred, whom he'd captured when he confiscated the castle he found, wasn't shy about giving his opinion. He also didn't blubber and cry like Luc's other prisoners.

"*I'm hungry.*"

23

"When can I go home?"

"You monster."

Sob.

Was it any wonder he threatened to tear out their tongues if they didn't stop?

Luc paced in front of the bars. "These stores of which you speak… How do they work? Do I simply enter and advise the shopkeeper of my needs?"

"Not quite. You are expected to choose your own items and bring them to the checkout."

"Carry the goods, as well?" Did these so-called stores not provide any service?

"Most have carts for you to use."

"With cattle to pull them?" Seemed kind of odd. Just how big were these shopping places?

"No, metal carts with wheels. You push them."

"Push? As in labor?" Luc sneered. He was quite good at it, especially once he'd discovered a properly given sneer or scowl got people to obey.

"It's not that hard." Alfred shook his head. "You really haven't the slightest clue, do you, boy?"

Boy? The disrespect was enough to make him bare his teeth.

"Put those things away. And stop breathing so hard. When was the last time you gargled some mouthwash? Not everyone wants to smell your last meal, you know. And would it kill you to use soap when you shower?"

Luc sealed his lips and glared.

"Don't be sulking now. You want to fit in, I'm telling you how."

"There are too many rules in your world." A vast amount of things for a former prisoner to learn.

"You know, it would be a lot easier for us both if you let me out of here so I could help you."

"Don't you mean try and kill me? I did, after all, overthrow your previous master."

"You did us all a favor. My previous employer was a pompous arse."

"So why didn't you kill him?"

"Because one does not simply murder people."

"Why not?"

"Because there are laws."

"Laws are for peasants." Or so his father had explained before he went on his final walk to feed the evil suzerain.

"This isn't the Dark Ages anymore, boy. We live in enlightened times where there are laws that apply to all, rich or poor."

"Not kings."

"Even kings."

But who made the laws to rule the kings? He smiled. "Then I shall be an emperor."

"That might be kind of difficult, given the current rulers of the countries won't agree to bow down to a stranger."

"Then I will kill them."

"Will you murder everyone who doesn't agree?"

"Probably." What else did he have to do? He'd promised his mother vengeance. However, Luc had yet to find Voadicia, and this dimension was much bigger and more populous than he ever imagined.

"That's a lot of dead people. And blood." Alfred set his cup down. "You'll need a manservant to ensure that your uniform of doom is kept clean and presentable. A ruler should look the part." Alfred shot him a look that held a touch of disdain.

Luc peered down at his ensemble, pilfered from a closet. The flowered blouse screamed of wealthy color— look at the patterns and all the different dyes used! The flowing skirt reminded him of the ceremonial robes his mother had described when rocking him to sleep. A mirrored reflection wasn't needed for Luc to recognize he looked splendid.

"When I venture forth, I strike awe in the hearts of those who behold me." They gave him a wide berth, recognizing his greatness.

"You look like a buffoon. Trust me when I say you need help."

"And how do I know you're to be trusted?"

"You have so much to learn." Alfred sighed and stood. He approached the bars, stuck his hand through, and tapped the oddly lit box on the front. The light went from red to green, and the human pushed on the bars. The door swung open, and Luc frowned.

"You know magic!"

"Not exactly." Alfred pointed at the box. "Electronic lock. All you need is the combination. These stalls weren't meant to hold people, but livestock."

"A dungeon for animals?" If only his previous quarters had been as spacious and clean.

"Not a dungeon but a stable. The previous owner raised horses."

"What are horses?"

"Four-legged steeds. Tall as you, taller in some cases. Covered in hair."

"I saw none of those in here." When he'd arrived, the huge, aboveground dungeon was bare.

"The horses were gone before you arrived."

"Why?"

"Does it really matter? They're gone, and the point I was trying to make is that I was never actually a prisoner. I could have left anytime I wanted. How else do you think I got fed?"

"I thought there were servants doing that task."

"You locked up all the servants."

"Speaking of whom, why are they quiet? On the previous occasions I entered, they emasculated themselves, begging for release."

"I let them go."

"You released my prisoners?" Luc drew himself tall and glared at Alfred, who, though hunched and old, wasn't that much shorter.

"Don't worry. I lied and told them you were playing a prank. Told them you were the previous castle owner's nephew and then gave them some money, along with a warning to say nothing to the coppers."

Sounded quite efficient, and explained the lack of screaming. Best of all, Luc didn't have to deal with any of it. Good thing, because he'd been at a loss for what to do. He focused on the last thing Alfred said. "You know the Copper dragons?"

"Coppers, as in police. Those who enforce the laws."

"Perhaps we should call them since you admit to stealing from the larders! No wonder the shelves are bare. It would serve you right if I sent you to the market to replace the items you removed." Then, he wouldn't have to go.

"I'll go, but only if you admit you need me," Alfred stated.

"Me, need you?" Luc scoffed. "I have no need of a

human's aid." Pride made him say it even as he heard his father admonishing him to take all the help he could get.

"You can cut the crap with me, sir." Luc liked the sound of the *sir* bit. "It's obvious you're not from around here, and I'm not going to ask where or why. That's your business. But you're obviously someone. And you need help. I can provide that."

"Exactly what are you suggesting?"

"Shopping, for one, since you're so adverse. But also teaching you how to fit in."

The man sought employment, but Luc remained skeptical. "Why? Why would you help me?"

Alfred shrugged. "Why not? I'm old and not in the mood to retire, but at the same time, who will hire me? I've got no kin left to speak of. And now that you've rid me of my previous employer, no purpose."

"I have a purpose." Revenge, followed by ruling the world.

"You do, but at the rate you're going, you'll never achieve it. You have much to learn if you're going to survive."

Luc rubbed his chin. "You wish to be my advisor?"

The human nodded.

While his first impulse was to scoff at the help—after all, even in his dimension, he'd heard of the barbaric humans from another plane—he held his tongue. It would seem the knowledge Luc had of humans was outdated. They'd grown since their last contact with his dimension. Evolved, and could now prove useful in his quest for revenge against the dragons.

Luc smiled. "Very well, consider yourself my advisor. As your first task, I need you to fetch me supplies from the village." Because he was hungry, and the cold box in the kitchen didn't magically replenish itself.

At least the hot water in the bathing chamber seemed never-ending. As well as the flow of fluid from things the old man called faucets.

No more visiting the well room with that massive hole in the ground. Long, thick chains dropped down the deep shaft. Each held a huge, steel bucket. It took more than a few bodies using all their strength to haul them to the top of the chute, the edges slick and slippery. There'd been a few incidents.

The drawing of water once the rivers went dry was a thankless chore reserved for the children, enslaved and prodded to go faster by the overseers. The underage prison gangs banded together and heaved on the chains, trying not to stumble on the wet stone. Since the hole in the ground had swallowed six—their screams a chilling echo as they fell—they'd tethered the front of the chain to the wall. The suzerain had wanted her water for her bath. Never mind that she could have used magic to do it. She enjoyed watching them suffer.

The suzerain was a vile dragon who needed to be found so Luc could end her miserable life. She, more than any other, was the reason his world had died. Why he was all alone.

Some of the blame also rested on her blubbery minions. Those two corpulent pustules upon his world might have hidden Luc from her notice and finally freed him from his prison; however, they shared the blame with Voadicia. They would be held accountable.

Vengeance: it kept Luc going since his hopes for a future and a progeny had been dashed because of a mad dragon's quest to live forever.

But was it really over for him? *I could breed and keep my line alive.*

With a human? At best, he'd father half-breeds. If it even worked. They were such a fragile race. Prone to weakness.

What of dragons?

He knew it was possible to mate successfully with them. Some of those imprisoned centuries after their arrival were hybrids. Those halflings hadn't been spared when the suzerain needed their life force to sustain herself.

However, breeding with a dragon would mean forgiving what they'd done.

Never.

He'd rather die alone than mate with a dragon.

Chapter Three

"Are you sure you're not available to mate?" Joanna—the Emerald Sept representative—asked yet again.

Babette shook her head. "Sorry. Now that the Golden one is back, I don't have to pop out babies." On account that they now could successfully mate with humans.

It used to be that humans and dragons made sterile male wyverns. However, with the return of the Golden dragon and with the help of magic, they could now perform the ritual to turn wyverns into full dragons. It just took time—and money.

The Silver Sept knew how to earn coins for the crown. Charging families to elevate wyverns to full status meant big bucks.

But the true power and wealth lay in arranged marriages. Babette, being the daughter of a Silvergrace, those chosen to be the king's left and right hands, was a coveted prize.

Elspeth didn't have such esteemed roots, and yet she

felt as if she should let Joanna know of her availability. "I'm single." Elspeth waved her hand. However, Joanna, in obvious need of glasses and a hearing aid, didn't notice.

"I have a nephew, late twenties, good teeth, impeccable hygiene. He would be perfect for you."

"Does he have a hole in the middle? I like my partners without the sausage, if you get what I mean." Babette freely announced her preference.

Joanna didn't even blink. "In that case, I've got a niece you might like."

"Stop throwing bodies at me. Not interested." Babette was being so polite when what she probably really wanted to say was that she still found herself heartbroken that Elspeth had chosen to gently rebuff her advances.

Perhaps I should revise my stance. Babette is a lovely catch, after all. Yet Elspeth couldn't muster more than a friendly liking that didn't resemble lust in the least.

"If you change your mind…" Joanna smiled, her entire demeanor friendly.

Elspeth found it a refreshing change from the grumpy Silver and Blue Septs with their haughty airs and perpetual frowns. Not to mention their threats every time she tried to hug a smile out of them. They obviously hadn't received enough affection as children.

"If we're done trying to marry me off, could we get back to the reason we're here?" Babsy asked.

Elsie had chosen to give her bestie a nickname as cool as her own. Babsy complained about it, but Elspeth knew she secretly loved it, else why threaten to shave her curls?

"Ah, yes. False alarm," Joanna tittered. As a person who tittered often, Elspeth recognized it as being fake. "I am terribly sorry you flew all this way. We tried to contact the king and cancel our request for aid, but you'd already set out. It seems it was all a misunderstanding."

"Humor me, would you? I mean, we're here, and we'll still have to write a report to justify the expenses." Babette smiled, and yet Elspeth noted it didn't reach her eyes. "Why don't we start with you explaining what exactly people saw in the sky?"

"They saw a dragon."

"Really? Because your initial report to the king indicated it was most definitely not a dragon."

"It turns out we were wrong. Seems it was one of our younger members sneaking out at night. A trick of the light made it seem like something different than it was."

Elspeth cocked her head with interest since it was very clear Joanna was lying.

"Tell me about the dragons who went missing." Babsy might have pretended to nap on the flight over, but had obviously found some time to read up on the mission. Gold star for her bestie!

"No one missing. Just young'uns who put a scare into us all. Testing their boundaries. Part of some weird social media game they play. Something called forty-eight hours." There was that false titter again.

More lying. Elspeth might have said something; however, Babette already wore a frown and questioned some more.

"What of the humans? Did they return, as well?"

Joanna shrugged, her appearance slick. "How would

I know? And why would I care? Humans go missing all the time. Since when is that our concern?"

"As a representative for the crown, I think we should all be concerned about the plight of humans who go wandering because they don't have owners to care for them. Have you thought about adopting one? I can hook you up with a doctor who can spay or neuter them, so you don't have to worry about adopting out babies." Elspeth smiled.

Joanna gaped before turning to Babette. "Is she for real?"

"Unfortunately. Back to the teens who went missing and came back. I'd like to speak with them."

"They've nothing to say."

"I'll be the judge of that."

Joanna's brow creased. "Are you implying something?"

Elspeth jumped in to ease the situation. "What my bestie means to say is that her mind would be greatly eased if she could see for herself that the teens in question were, in fact, off experiencing life and not the victims of a predator."

"It wasn't just teens." Joanna's chin tilted. "I was one of those who went missing. And I assure you, I am fine. Nothing happened. I just needed some time alone."

"Where did you go?"

"None of your business."

"Who did you go with?" Babette fired another question.

Rising to her feet, Joanna's gaze turned icy. "I don't like your tone."

"I don't like your hair."

Babette and Joanna stood toe to toe, and Elspeth

could practically see the sexual energy simmering between them. What else to explain the irrational anger?

"Now, now, lovebirds. Let's take things down a notch. Joanna, you need to remember you're married, and while I realize you can't help being attracted to my bestie—she is, after all, quite the catch—you will have to restrain yourself. It's unseemly."

"I am not—"

"Are you insane—?"

Ah, the protests. Elspeth nodded, keeping her smug smile to herself. She was so good at reading people.

Joanna's lips pressed into a tight line. "I think we're done."

"No, we're not." Babette shook her head. She did it so often it probably explained the smoothness of her neck. Elspeth tended to nod in agreement, which she believed helped prevent multiple chins.

"There is nothing for you to investigate. Return to the USA and tell your king—"

"He's not just mine, he's yours, too," Elspeth declared. "He is the Golden one, the dragon foretold. After centuries of waiting, he has returned to guide his loyal subjects."

"He's not the only choice out there," Joanna remarked, referencing Samael, the half-dragon, and Brand, the genetically created one.

"Only Remiel is the true Golden king. The others lack his purity. His—"

Joanna's lips pulled into a sneer. "He is a stranger and a possible madman. Why else would Parker and the Crimson Sept have held him prisoner? They obviously knew something about your king."

"Like what?" Babette asked.

"I guess we'll never know since Parker and most of the upper Crimson echelon are dead. Convenient, I'd say," Joanna uttered dryly.

"Are you implying that he murdered them?" Elspeth couldn't help a high note. "Our king is the most honorable dragon there is."

"Is he?"

Elspeth struggled to keep her smile. *Don't frown. Don't get mad. Remember what happens when you get angry.* A good thing she'd taken her pills that morning.

"Let's go, Elsie." Babette grabbed her by the arm and dragged her toward the door. "This cow is obviously deranged and a traitor."

"Cow?" Joanna screeched. "Why you inbred Silver bitch. Get out and don't come back."

Despite Joanna acting out because she couldn't have Babette, and the fact that the Emerald doubted their king's rule, Elspeth knew the right thing to do. "Glad to meet you and even happier that all is fine with your Sept. Should you require aid in the future, we would be delighted to provide assistance." They may not provide it in a timely fashion, however.

The door firmly slammed shut behind them, cutting off any lingering goodbyes, which was very responsible of the Emerald dragoness as it would keep out the drafts that would drive up the home heating expenses. Mother had explained that to Elspeth after an unsuccessful bout of door-to-door knocking requesting donations for a worthy cause. Namely, the eradication of toilet paper to save the environment. It didn't prove popular, and even Elspeth had abandoned the idea when the leaves she'd gathered left a rash on her tushie.

"What a cow that woman is. Treating us like crap." Babette whirled on the door and lifted her foot.

"It's not the door that should be punished." Elspeth grabbed the foot before it could connect and tugged her bestie down the steps.

Babsy had great balance, and hopped along, keeping up. "What the hell, Elsie? I need to kick that cow's ass."

"I realize your attraction to Joanna is great. Your anger for each other made that clear. However, we did not come to Ireland to wreck her marriage. Although, if her husband were to suffer an unfortunate accident…"

"Are you insane?"

"Not according to the asylum Mother sent me to." They'd poked and prodded her. Given her all kinds of colored pills. But in the end, once she'd learned what to say, they'd declared her normal with a heightened state of optimism. A real ray of sunshine—which, for some reason, made her mother cry.

"Sometimes I wonder about you, Elsie."

She used to wonder about her sanity, too. People thought her blind to what happened around her. She saw it, saw more than they imagined. She just preferred to look at the lighter side. The positive.

She had to because of the darkness… Stay away from it.

Happy face. Elspeth beamed at Babette. "I am delighted to hear you've been wondering about me, bestie. I wonder about you, too."

"Don't worry. I'm already certifiably insane. All the doctors agree. Which means, anything I do can be blamed on my condition. My mom's lawyers got those ducks in a row years ago." Babette yanked her foot free and turned to head back to the house.

Elspeth tripped her. "While your infatuation with Joanna is adorable, perhaps you should look for someone more available. Unless you want to kill her husband, in which case, as your bestie, I'd have to help you hide the body."

"For the last time, I am not attracted to that cow. I want to question her some more. My gut says that woman is hiding something."

"Do you think she's a man?" Elsie's eyes widened.

"No. I mean hiding information about the whole missing people thing."

"You heard what she said. The dragons all returned."

"Says her. I say, let me talk to them and prove they're alive."

"And if they are? What then?"

"Then I ask where they went. I didn't believe her for one minute when she said she went off for some alone time."

"Perhaps she and the others are part of a secret club. Or a bunch of them went on vacation and didn't want someone to know." That happened quite often to Elsie. People did such a good job of making their trips and parties a surprise that they forgot to tell her. Looking at the pictures and videos afterwards was almost like being there.

"I'm telling you, Elsie, I think those sneaky Emeralds are hiding something. And I don't like it."

"I think someone needs a hug."

Babsy held up a hand as Elspeth moved in with arms outstretched.

"Don't you dare. My ribs just healed from the last time."

"A good thing we discovered your need for extra calcium to strengthen those bones."

"I'm a dragon. We don't need milk."

"Nonsense. Milk does the body good. Speaking of which, I could really use a carton of chocolate milk. Can we hit a store on the way back to the hotel?"

Babette's nose wrinkled "You hit the store. I'm going to find a bar where the drinks are huge and not watered down."

"Alas, I'm afraid I cannot join you due to my allergy to alcohol." Elsie had imbibed only three times in her life. Each time, the result wasn't pretty. And, really, with her condition, she shouldn't drink. It only made it worse.

"What a pity. Guess I'll see you back at the hotel. Eventually," Babette muttered, splitting away from Elsie.

"Bye, bestie. Have fun." She was so happy Babette didn't allow her unrequited affection for the Emerald dragon to keep her down.

One day, she hoped to find someone who made her giddy with love. Thus far, Elspeth had yet to meet a man who could handle her exuberance. She'd promised Mother after she broke the first one to be more careful. She'd made that same promise the second and third times, too. Now, even the cops were keeping an eye on her.

Wanting to avoid arrest because men were so fragile meant passing on many opportunities. However, she didn't let that discourage her. One day, her dragon prince would come. She totally believed it, and yet her dreams always showed her someone darker and more dangerous. His face was hidden from her, as was his name. She only ever saw his eyes, those blazing blue orbs with a hint of red in the middle.

Entering a grocery store, Elspeth couldn't help but smile at everyone she saw as she wandered the aisles, basket over her arm.

At the checkout, with her several cartons of chocolate milk and a wheel of cheese, she noticed an elderly gent with a cart full of groceries. All alone, the poor thing.

She followed him out to the parking lot and got close to him—in case he was deaf—before saying, "Let me help you with that."

The poor fellow tucked a hand inside the breast of his jacket as he whirled. Obviously suffering from a weak ticker. Good thing she'd come along. He would have probably collapsed of a heart attack otherwise.

"I'm fine," he declared.

"Nonsense. I've got this. You sit in the car while I handle it." She shoved him in the direction of the driver's seat and then proceeded to stow the groceries. Mostly meat. Hardly any veggies. And ice cream. Lots and lots of chocolate ice cream. She liked ice cream.

When done, she tapped on his window. He rolled it down and peered at her. "Ma'am?"

She giggled. "That's my mother. I'm Elsie. Just so you know, all your groceries are in the trunk of your car."

"Thank you."

"That was an awful lot of food. Is there someone at home to help you bring it in?"

"I'll be fine."

Which was code for he was alone. "Lucky for you, I have nothing to do this evening."

Before the man could thank her, she placed her bag on the floor and sat in the passenger seat.

The old fellow gaped at her.

Since that happened quite often, she smiled and held out her hand. "Elspeth Canard. A pleasure to meet you." She introduced herself more properly. At his age, he probably didn't remember the first time she did it.

"Erm, Alfred."

"Hi, Erm. I assume it's all right to call you that, or would you prefer Mr. Alfred?"

"Just Alfred will suffice."

"Well, Alfred, shall we?" She placed her hands on her knees, her skirt tucked over them. She wore a vivid emerald number this evening, with black cloverleaves for contrast and a white boat collar.

Babette had choked with envy. The velvet green chunky heels with black buckles were almost as epic as her lipstick—Plump Cherry Delight.

"Miss, you can't come with me. What if something happens? People will have seen us on the security cameras."

"See, even you're worried something will happen. It's settled. I'm going with you.

"I am surely out of your way."

"I've got nothing better to do. And don't worry about driving me back. I'll call a taxi."

"The master won't like this," he muttered.

"You have a master? How lovely." Being a woman of the world, Elsie didn't ask him to elaborate. She'd seen *Fifty Shades of Grey*; however, she did have a hard time picturing Alfred in leather chaps being spanked. Or was he the spanker?

She'd soon find out. Since he sat there not moving, she gently prodded. "Would you like me to drive?" She didn't have a license anymore. Apparently, parking her car across the middle of a highway and forcing traffic to stop—for miles—to help a family of ducks cross was a major infraction, but she'd been in a different country. Surely, those same rules didn't apply here.

And driving the elderly was a public service.

"I've got this," he mumbled, putting the car in gear. "But Master Luc won't like this. Mark my words."

She would have totally marked them if she had a pen that wrote on air. Someone should totally invent one.

Chapter Four

This invention is incredible.

A picture frame, and a rather sizeable one at that, somehow captured entire places and people and put them inside to act for his personal pleasure.

When Alfred showed him how to press a button and activate the magic of the object Alfred called a telly-vision, Luc had jumped and punched, breaking the first one. But the castle he'd commandeered had others, and he'd learned to watch the screen rather than pulverize it.

Only one of the many things he'd learned. He'd discovered toilets for depositing waste—that…flushed. A cold box with food like pizza. He really liked pizza, and even knew how to make it himself. The oven that required no coal or kindling heated it to crispy perfection, and while he ate the gooey, savory slice, he watched the telly-vision. Watched wide-eyed in amazement, barely sleeping. He learned so much.

Discounted quite a bit, as well. He didn't believe most of the plays he saw. Especially the size of the futuristic cities with their gleaming, tall buildings that stretched impossibly into the sky. The castle he lived in was made of stone, as expected, much like the ruin he'd exited into when he left his home world.

Impossibly tall and narrow spires of glass? A fantasy, surely.

Alfred tried to convince him that it was real, as were the milling people on the streets, and the thick lines of cars during something he'd called a traffic jam.

Luc saw no evidence of jam anywhere, just the noisy carriages. The steedless chariots ran because of something Alfred had called science. Using machines. And combustion. Fancy words for a different kind of magic.

In this world, away from the prison that quelled his power, he could feel some of the things his mother had tried to explain. The almost river-like sensation of magic running over him. He only had to raise a metaphysical hand to tap into it.

He trailed his fingers only along the very edges and shuddered at the potential there. But was it too much? He'd only ever had access to crumbs of power while in the cell. Barely enough to create a spark. Only just enough for his mother to teach him.

Now, there was too much, and he feared glutting himself on it. Magic could take a toll.

You're scared to use it.

He ignored the voice. It sounded like his mother. But she was dead.

I taught you how to harness it.

Small puddles, not torrential rivers with strong currents.

We came from this world. We were made to handle it.

Perhaps the ability to control weakened over time

from disuse. Perhaps the magic, with no one using it, got wildly out of control.

He left the magic alone but constantly remained aware of it. A good thing because something disturbed it. There was a shiver in the magical river, and an easing of its current.

Luc noticed it immediately and straightened. He sat in the parlor, watching a woman extoll on the features of a silver chain and dangling pendant. Luc wondered why anyone would want something they were selling ten thousand copies of. He watched them flying off the shelf, the inventory number decreasing. Fools, paying to be one of the flock.

He'd rather be unique.

He also wanted to be left alone. Which, apparently, wasn't happening. He heard voices coming from the kitchen. Which was odd, considering he'd gotten rid of all his other prisoners. The only one he'd kept was Alfred.

Well, Alfred and some cleaners. The old fellow claimed scrubbing floors and doing dishes was beneath him. But the crew Alfred hired had left for the day, so why did he hear a feminine voice?

He crept down the hall, silent in his bare feet, listening for clues.

"This is a cool castle, Alfred. Is it just you and your master living here?"

"I am not at liberty to divulge my master's business." The words emerged stiffly.

The reply to it was soft and lilting. "Oh, I get it. Still in the closet about your relationship. Totally cool. But just so you know, I am down with it. No judgment from me."

"I think you misunderstand, miss."

"You don't have to explain, Alfie. Where is your freezer for the ice cream?"

The rustle of bags, thumping of cupboard doors, and the distinct hiss of the seal being broken on the cooling unit filled the next few minutes.

Luc crept closer. The feminine voice was quite fascinating and, at the same time, irritating with its cheerfulness.

What reason does she have to be so happy?

He peered around the edge of the doorway into the kitchen and saw nothing but Alfred, perched on a stool, looking bemused. His manservant caught sight of him, and Luc mouthed, "What's going on?"

The old man shrugged before saying aloud, "Do you always help random strangers?"

A voice echoed from the freezer. "My mother says helping those weaker than me is a waste of time, but I like providing aid to people. It makes me feel good."

Altruism to feel good? Luc's lip curled.

"A young lady like yourself should be more careful about offering her services. You might find yourself caught in a bad situation."

Rich laughter boomed, and it made Luc shudder. When was the last time he'd had a reason to indulge in mirth?

"Oh, Alfie. You flirt. I might look dainty, but I assure you, I'm tougher than I look."

The voice grew in volume as the unknown woman neared the door to the cooling unit. Luc popped back before she could see him.

He'd gotten enough of the gist of the situation to realize that a stranger had offered Alfred some aid.

But why? Surely, she lied about her charitable tendencies. More likely, she was a spy sent by his enemies to ferret out his intentions. Yet, he'd have sworn no one suspected his presence. An erroneous assumption. Perhaps, at this very moment, his enemies reconnoitered and gathered for an attack.

Let them try. He'd fight and refuse to surrender to his very last breath.

"All done, Alfie. Anything else I can help you with?"

"No, you've done more than enough."

"It was so nice meeting you."

"Ack."

Luc's eyes widened as he heard the pop of bones cracking. The female dared to kill his servant?

He popped his head around the corner to look, only to squeak—in a manner much like the rodents he'd hunted in his old cell—when a pair of vivid green eyes met his.

A bright voice chirped, "Hi, you must be Alfred's master. You're younger than I expected."

"You are trespassing," he managed to mutter in reply, which was more than he'd thought possible given the way she'd startled him.

It didn't help that her very appearance stunned him. Her hair gleamed the golden yellow of a brilliant sun and hung in short, bouncy curls. Her skin appeared slightly tanned as if kissed by the sun's rays. Freckles scattered across her straight nose. Her lips, full and red, juicy and plump, curved into a smile. Eyes the vivid green of the grass outside shone as she stared at him inquisitively.

It wasn't only her face that stunned him. She stood a handspan shorter than him. A novelty, given all the females he'd encountered thus far in this dimension tended toward the shorter stature. She was broad of shoulder and muscled. Strong. Not some weak-fleshed female, and she was definitely all woman.

He couldn't help but notice her generous, hour-glass shape. Her hips were full, her waist indented; the skirt she wore belling and falling demurely to her knees. As for her breasts, they were indecently embraced by the form-fitting top of her gown, the round collar displaying her slender neck from the shoulders up.

Given her rather inappropriate attire—a woman showing her calves and her neck—his cock stirred, aroused by this…this…gorgeous female. It raised his ire.

"Get out." He practically growled the command.

Her eyes widened with clear chagrin. "Oh, dear. I've made you jealous. I'm so sorry. Let me assure you that Alfred was nothing but a gentleman with me. Nothing inappropriate happened, so there is no reason for you to be angry with him. He's still one hundred percent yours."

Her words made no sense, but her smell… He inhaled again and sifted past the honeyed fragrance surrounding her to the baser one underneath. He knew that smell.

"You're a dragon," he snarled. The enemy in his home. Confronting him. He drew taller and expanded his chest.

"My, what a good sense of smell you have. I am a dragon." She clapped her hands, her smile bright. "Can you guess what color? I'll give you a hint. It's rare. So rare, my daddy accused my mother of cheating on him. But it turns out, after the paternity test was done, that there have been others like me that've popped up from time to time in his line."

Her babbling was obviously meant to confuse him. However, he didn't let himself forget the fact that she'd tracked him down.

He squinted at her. "What are you doing here?"

"Helping Alfred with the groceries."

"You're spying on me!" he declared. "Have you come to finish the annihilation of my race?"

"Race? I didn't know we were competing. I'm not really wearing the right footwear for it." She peered down at her shoes, green with large buckles, the toes peeking—the tips of them a shade of pink that would look better around his ears. Not a position he'd indulged in yet in this world; however, he'd seen it in a play on the telly-vision that went into graphic sexual detail. Alfred called it porn. He called it enlightening.

She slid off her shoe and wiggled her foot. "Can we race barefoot to make it even?" She sought to obscure the issue. Obviously, a special talent of hers.

"No matter your plan, I will fight it. I won't be captured and imprisoned again."

"Poor thing." She reached out and patted his cheek, creating an electrical shock that caused him to recoil. "Did someone cage you? Are you another of Parker's victims? He put my second cousin Tomas in a cell. Mother says that didn't end well for those who did it."

"What do you know of those incarcerated?"

"Not much. Everyone is always trying to protect me from the ugly things in the world." She leaned forward to whisper. "They think I'm fragile."

Her, fragile? "They are obviously blind."

"And you're cute, which is probably one of the

reasons you were put in a cage." She patted his cheek again, and he turned his head, snapping his teeth, but missed her flesh. "You also smell really good. Like a hot cinnamon stick. Yummy. I just want to lick you all over." Her eyes widened as she admitted her dark desire, and her cheeks turned a rosy shade.

He didn't let her escape the truth. "You admit to feasting on my kind?" What a stroke of chance finding one of Voadicia's minions.

"Eat you?" She eyed him up and down, her gaze lingering on a spot below his waist that only served to make his cock swell larger. "While you are ridiculously tempting, I would never think to come between you and Alfred. Although I might be talked into a threesome." She winked before whirling and flouncing back into the kitchen proper.

Meanwhile, he tried to process her statement. A threesome as in him, her, and…Alfred? The thought of getting into bed with the old fellow shriveled his cock, allowing the blood in his body to pump to his other extremities and organs, such as the starving brain in his head. He snapped out of his surprise enough to notice the woman with her hand on the back door.

"Where do you think you're going?" he boomed.

"I am returning to my hotel before my chocolate milk goes bad. It was nice meeting you both. I hope you have many happy years together. Toodles." She waggled her fingers before exiting.

For a moment, he stared at the door, stunned. A dragon, here in his home. An attractive one. A woman who had seen him and was leaving! Probably to report his presence.

Taking long strides, Luc hurried after her, making it

to the kitchen door and flinging it open in time to see her changing shape, a brilliant yellow dragon—not gold, or any other shade, but yellow—taking to the sky with a grocery sack in her clawed hand. She uttered a trilling noise that could only be an ominous warning.

Luc whirled on Alfred. "Who is she? Where did you find her?"

"She claims her name is Elspeth. Elsie for short. She was at the same market as me and insisted on providing aid given my advanced years."

"She called you weak?"

"Not exactly, sir. In this time, it is considered respectful to aid those more senior with chores."

"Treat them as invalids more like. Are you an invalid, Alfred?"

"No, sir."

"Good, because in my world, when the weak could no longer care for themselves, they volunteered their lives to the suzerain to spare those with more able bodies."

"I've still got plenty of strength left to serve, sir."

"Good, because I have need of you, Alfred."

The old man straightened. "What does my master require? I replenished the freezer with ice cream as requested."

"Really?" For a moment, Luc forgot the yellow dragoness in favor of recollecting how the cold treat melted in his mouth, creating a groaningly pleasant experience that he couldn't get enough of.

"Would you like a bowl, sir?"

Yes. But duty came first. Luc shook his head. "No. We must prepare, Alfred."

"Prepare for what, sir?"

"Guests. Uninvited ones. It won't be long before that female returns with her companions. We must ready for attack. Arm the defenses," he barked. "Load the catapults. Boil the cauldrons of oil. Ready the archers."

"Er, sir, we have no weaponry."

Startled, Luc paused in his pacing. "What do you mean, we have no weapons? What kind of castle is this? How am I supposed to defend against my enemies?"

"Perhaps you are mistaken. I don't think the girl meant you any harm."

"Shows how little you know about dragons." They were evil creatures. Who cared what the stories on his moving picture box claimed? Train them, indeed.

Not the dragons he knew. They came to his world, centuries before his birth. Pretended friendship. Then stole his people's secrets and perverted them.

When the dragons could no longer hide their actions, they imprisoned Luc's people. To which, Luc always asked, "Why didn't you fight?"

And his father's reply? "We were banished to that realm for our violent natures. We overcame our primal impulses to build a society. To fight would have been to turn our backs on that achievement."

"But you became slaves."

"Better slaves than a return to the monsters we once were."

A logic that had led to the extinction of Luc's people.

I am the only one left, and I don't care what my father or his ancestors thought. I won't allow myself to be a victim. Not anymore.

Despite the lack of crossbows, the castle did have

one ancient sword hanging on the wall in the great room.

Taking to the ramparts, Luc sharpened the old, pitted blade and watched the sky. He remained sentinel —with a cup of hot cocoa and a plate of cookies Alfred had brought—as night turned back into day.

The dawning blue sky showed not a speck marring it.

Nothing appeared by air or by land, not even a stunningly beautiful dragoness with a smile and speech meant to confuse. With a scent that aroused, rather than repelled. Probably part of a spell to muddle his senses.

A potent hex since he couldn't forget her.

Someone cleared their throat. "Ahem. Would the master like me to draw him a warm bath? Your bones are probably chilled from spending the night outdoors."

A bath did sound pleasant. Perhaps it would ease his disappointment, which he felt surely as a result of a battle not ensuing—and not because his balls ached.

However, the steamy basin of water did nothing to ease the tension in his groin. He shagged himself, spending his seed and achieving a measure of relief that lasted but a moment. He only had to close his eyes and picture a dancing green gaze to harden again.

How utterly irritating, and evidence of one crucial thing.

I need a female.

A real female—preferably with blonde hair—and not his hand to sate his needs.

"Alfred?" he bellowed, and his manservant, towel in hand, immediately answered.

"Yes, sir."

"I wish to purchase the services of a courtesan."

"Not too many of those around here, sir, but given you're a handsome fellow, might I suggest a local tavern where the women are often receptive to masculine attention if you buy them a few drinks."

"A tavern?" He'd never been to one but had heard stories of them and seen hints of what Alfred spoke of on the moving picture box. He'd also never drunk alcohol. Their prison didn't provide more than the basics for sustenance—barely.

"Yes, a tavern. There's a place not too far from the castle. Perhaps you'll have luck finding a woman there."

Luc rose from the tub, water streaming from his limbs. "That is a fine idea, Alfred. I shall go at once."

"Perhaps you might want to rest first. The taverns don't begin truly having patrons of the kind you're seeking until after the dinner hour."

Rest after a night spent awake and watching did sound good. "Very well. Keep watch upon the ramparts whilst I sleep, Alfred. Sound the alarm if the enemy approaches."

No one appeared to disturb his rest, which meant that he slept the day away. Only as dusk fell did Luc find himself at the door to a tavern, dressed in a strange material Alfred called denim and a soft shirt that hugged his chest rather intimately. He lacked any kind of protective gear.

Alfred wouldn't let him wear any armor, even though the metal suit he'd found in the upper gallery fit him, if tightly. His servant also gave him a few tips on dealing with women of this world. The old man ticked them off one by one on his fingers before dropping him off.

"Remember to compliment them. Offer to buy them a drink. Ask them if they are on birth control."

"Humans can't easily sire children with my kind." Or so he was taught.

"You might also want to refrain from referring to them as *humans*," Alfred advised before Luc stepped out of the metal carriage with the noisy steeds under the hood.

"Peasants?"

"No."

Luc sighed. "This lack of respect for their betters is tiring."

"You aren't ruling the world yet, sir. I would suggest being covert until you do."

"You are wise for a human, Alfred."

"Thank you, sir. Here, take this." Alfred handed over the bits of paper he'd claimed would act as wealth. A flimsy wealth that would never survive a fire like pure metal could.

He stuffed the paper into his pocket and entered the tavern with its raucous noise. Luc gaped at the bawdy place.

Gloomy, only a few dim lights illuminated the tavern with its high tables and stools. Music, with a hard thump that vibrated his bones, filled the room. The volume of it kept him from hearing the many conversations taking place because the tavern found itself overly occupied.

By courtesans! They were everywhere, wearing short and tight garments that exposed most of their legs. They wore brilliant face paint. Some had even grown out their claws—which he'd never known the human females could do—and colored them.

The males, of all types, young and old, were dressed

much like he was, and most of them conducted business with the courtesans.

I've come to the right place.

Now to pick out a female to satisfy his carnal needs.

A few steps in, his cock went ramrod hard, and he exclaimed, "You!"

Chapter Five

"You, come with me."

The woman proved amenable to joining him outside. The door, marked in glowing letters as *Exit*, led into an alley, the smell not as fresh as the green, grassy fields he liked to bury the bodies in.

The female draped her arms around his neck, wrapping him tightly, her lips, coated with a colored wax, pressed to his. The alcohol she'd imbibed was strong enough to ignite.

He allowed her to embrace him, even to touch him, but he didn't reciprocate. He cast out his senses in search of anyone nearby that might spy on them.

Naught but the tiny flickers of rodent life, scurrying in search of dinner.

I'm hungry, too. Hungry enough that he didn't wait for home. He latched onto her mouth, but the taste wasn't the sweetness he craved. He hoisted her against the wall with one hand while the other fisted her yellow hair.

He drew her neck back and trailed his mouth over the skin, feeling the flutter of her pulse against his lips.

That excited him.

He held her pinned to the wall with his body to free a hand to unfasten his trousers. He shoved up her skirt.

She panted. "Yes. Yes."

The cries of encouragement continued when he entered her, a hard thrust then another as he continued to suck at the skin of her neck.

It didn't take him long to reach his peak.

To feel himself on the edge of spilling.

He struck, the body in his grasp stiffening, but not fighting. With a last soft exhale, she died in his arms, feeding him what he needed.

He sucked her dry then pulled away, letting her fall into a boneless heap on the ground.

He wiped the back of his hand across his mouth, removing the last stain of the waxen gloss she'd left on him.

A faint echo of voices at the end of the alley drew his sharp attention. They passed, and yet were a reminder that he'd acted out in the open. The evidence lay at his feet.

Not for long.

He twisted his hand, and a ball of flame danced on the palm. Dropping the flame onto the body ignited her hair and clothes.

By the time someone discovered the fire, it would be too late. The magical flames ate at the body until nothing was left but bones. Evidence of foul play, but nothing that would link back to him.

The deed done, he exited the alley to the entrance of the noisy establishment. Every time the door opened, a wave of sound emerged. He caught a glimpse of bodies. Bare skin. Delicious.

Those inside were safe for the moment, though. He'd sated his hunger.

Chapter Six

After a day spent watching the Emerald house—do nothing—Babette declared they needed to do something fun.

Elspeth suggested a movie. Babette dragged her to a tavern instead.

"This place is awfully tame," Babsy complained, giving the bar a side-eye. "Where's the mechanical bull? Or the cage dancers? Heck, there's not even a dance floor."

"Use your imagination," Elspeth prompted. "If you feel a need to kick up your heels, there's always the tables or the bartop."

"True." Babette eyed the scarred, wooden surfaces. "And now that we're here, I'll bet we can liven things up."

"That's the spirit," Elspeth exclaimed. "Look for the positive in every situation."

"More like get drunk until you don't care. Speaking of which, I need something in a frosted mug. What do you want?"

"Water, please," Elspeth said.

"Water?" Babs sounded aghast. "This is a bar, not a gym. Screw that healthy shit."

"I don't drink alcohol. It doesn't agree with me."

"Then how about a soda?"

Elspeth shook her head. "I can't ingest caffeine, either. I get hyper."

"You mean this is you au naturel?" Babette's mouth rounded. "Shit. That's scary. I'll be back. I need a drink because I, for one, am not allergic and could use one."

Off stomped her best friend, not pleased by the fact that the Emeralds weren't answering her calls for further discussion. Babette kept railing that there was something fishy about Joanna's explanation. Given her BFF's preoccupation with the Emeralds, Elspeth never had a chance to detail her encounter with the handsome man the day before.

A man who smelled yummy and different. Not human. Not shifter. Or dragon. Like nothing she'd ever encountered. And his eyes…they reminded her of her dreams.

A shame he was already in a committed relationship. He'd managed to pique her interest.

Since their meeting, she couldn't stop thinking about him. Remembering his electric presence. His short, dark hair. His stern expression that begged for her to do something, anything, to make those lips curve into a smile.

She wasn't kidding when she'd told him he smelled good enough to lick. And eat. And…

Thinking of him again was probably what triggered the memory of his smell. Cinnamon spice. All that was nice.

"You!"

Why, she even heard his voice.

"What are you doing here?" he barked before coming into view.

A bright smile burst forth. "Well, hello again."

"Are you following me?" he asked.

She blinked. "I don't think so."

"What do you mean you don't think so? Are you, or aren't you?"

"Well, I wasn't consciously planning to follow you, and yet, I have found my thoughts consumed by my recollection of our meeting. Therefore, it is possible on some subliminal level that my spirit, drawn to you, managed to decipher via the esoteric waves of fate where you would be and arranged for me to arrive before you."

He blinked. Long, dark lashes over those vivid eyes. "You are insane."

"Not according to my doctors." But she did hear that a lot. Mother claimed it was because her mind worked on a different level than everyone else's.

"I know what you're doing," he said, leaning in, bringing his mouthwatering scent close.

"What am I doing?" Because she hadn't the slightest clue. Good thing he knew, though. One of them should understand what was happening.

"You're trying to disarm me with your sexual appeal. Obviously, your words are some kind of spell meant to bedazzle me."

"They are?" Wow, she'd never known she had that ability. Weird visions. Freakish strength. Optimism. And now, a power to mesmerize handsome men. Or at least one man.

"Your magic spell won't work. I am telling you right now that my attraction to you will never come to fruition. I am strong enough to resist."

"I should hope you resist. Think of Alfred." It was what she did to prevent her hands from grabbing him and groping him inappropriately.

"Furthermore, you can tell your dragon superiors that I won't be easy to beat. I will have my revenge."

"Oooh. A vendetta. How awesome. Tell me more." She cupped her chin in her hands and prepared to listen intently.

He pulled away. "I am not revealing the details of my plan. Suffice it to say, it will be devious, and bloody."

"Sounds like fun. When does it start?"

His lips flattened. "I've already said too much. Stop following me." He turned, presenting a delicious view of his glutes as he strutted away, shouting, "Barkeep, a mug of your finest ale."

Babette chose that moment to return, sliding a glass with a lemon wedge and fizzing clear liquid at her. Her bestie had chosen a large tankard of a rather foul-looking beer with a thick froth on top as her beverage of choice.

Elspeth eyed her glass. "This isn't water."

"It's tonic water. The fancy version."

"I should probably stick to the regular kind."

"Okay." Babette's lower lip jutted. "I guess I'm a shitty friend for not listening."

"I'm being so ungrateful. I'm sorry. This is fine." Contrition had Elspeth taking a big swallow, the fizzing liquid a touch bitter, but she downed half the glass and smiled.

Babette returned her grin before sipping her

beverage of choice. "I gotta ask, where did you find that dress?"

"Custom-made, actually." Given her general height proved a disadvantage for off-the-rack shopping, Elspeth engaged the services of a seamstress for her fancier attire. The one she sported was a crisp white covered in glossy cherries, the collar hemmed in lace. The sleeves were tight, as was the waist before it belled into a pleated skirt that swung if she twirled.

"It would be killer if you wore it with stiletto heels."

"Sharp spikes and I don't get along." Not to mention at over six feet already, adding a few more inches tended to intimidate people.

"See any prospects worthy of getting under your skirt?" Babette asked, glancing at the crowd inside the bar.

Just one. "There is a guy."

"Really?" Babette rounded on her with rounded eyes. "What guy?"

"The yummy-smelling one I met yesterday."

"You met a guy? When? How?" Babsy hammered.

"Last night at his house."

"Please do not tell me you went to a strange guy's house alone without telling anyone."

"Okay."

"Okay, what?"

"I won't tell you."

Babette blinked. "You went, didn't you?"

Elspeth nodded.

"Did you blow him?"

"Babsy!" Her cheeks heated.

"No head? Can't blame you. I'm a pie girl myself.

Did you do the horizontal tango? Or is he a shifter into the doggy style?"

While Elspeth was a rather open person, reminding her of some of the fantasies she'd entertained about Alfred's master did make her squirm. Elspeth gulped more of her drink. It heated her from the inside out.

"You're not answering. Holy shit, you did do him?"

"No. Of course, not." Although she'd wanted to kiss him. Did that count? "He's already involved with someone."

"I'm gonna wager you can take her."

"You mean him. He's with a lovely older gent named Alfred."

"An old dude, eh? Probably wouldn't take much to get his ticker to explode. I can help if you want." Babsy took a large sip of her beer and licked the foam from her upper lip.

The fact that Babette wanted to help murder Alfred to clear the way warmed Elspeth's heart. "No need to remove anyone. Although I am really beginning to wonder about their relationship." She pointed her chin in his direction where he sat at the bar. "He's here."

"Which one is it?"

"The good-looking one. With the dark hair." Who'd just dragged a woman onto his lap. Elspeth's nails raked the tabletop.

"Well, well, looks like someone is a bit of a gigolo when his old man isn't around."

For some reason, this disappointed Elspeth. What-ever happened to true love and commitment? No wonder she was having such a hard time finding The One.

But she wouldn't give up. She finished off her fancy

water, and Babsy lifted her hand. A moment later, another glass found its way in front of Elspeth. She took a long draw via the straw as she glared in *his* direction.

She didn't even know his name. Probably because he was rude. He'd not introduced himself the day before. Or tonight. The rude jerk gallivanted about town, flirting with a lady while poor Alfred… She didn't know where Alfred was, but he surely wouldn't condone this behavior.

A good thing Alfred had Elspeth to champion him. She would give his *master* a piece of her mind. Really, cheating on dear, sweet Alfred like that. She took a long sip before getting up from the table.

"Where are you going?" Babsy asked.

"To talk to him."

"Good luck cock-blocking."

Moving closer, even with the music, she could hear the woman giggling. "You're funny."

"It was not my intention to be comical. My motive is purely sexual. I bought you a beverage. Indicated you are acceptably attractive. Shall we adjourn to somewhere more private so that I might perform coitus with you?"

Elspeth was shocked. More than shocked. Marching over, she stated, loudly enough for the human to hear, "Get away from him. He's practically a married man. And judging by the ring on your finger, you're also unavailable. You should both be ashamed." Elspeth wagged her finger at the pair.

The handsome devil scowled, making him more good-looking, whereas the woman on his lap frowned. "Who the fuck are you?"

"His conscience." Elspeth held herself tall.

"Nobody," was his reply.

The brunette sneered. "Why don't you fuck off, slut. This bloke is mine."

The woman turned her head to plaster her mouth to his, leaving Elspeth to gape.

Poor Alfred. Surely, chagrin at how the man was being treated was why she felt such rage.

Rage?

Oh, dear. Find your happy place. She tried. She truly did. However, that *woman*, that hussy, kept touching him.

Elspeth couldn't find a positive spin. Molten rage bubbled within, melting the effects of her pills and demanding an outlet. The hair-sprayed brown mess in front of her provided an outlet.

Before she knew it, Elspeth had her fingers wrapped in it, and she'd yanked the woman off his lap.

"What part of *he's taken* did you not grasp?" Elspeth grumbled as she dragged the screeching woman across the room.

Rip. Left with a handful of hair, she paused and turned to see the woman clutching at her much shorter style.

"Why, you fucking bitch. Do you have any idea what that weave cost me?"

"I'd be more concerned about the cost of your self-respect. And what of your marriage? Does no one honor their vows?" Elspeth asked aloud, raising her gaze heavenward. Except the answer wasn't to be found in the wood-paneled ceiling.

The cheating Jezebel took that moment to barrel into her, hitting Elspeth in the midsection and driving her into the bar.

Someone—known as Babette—began chanting. "Fight. Fight. Fight. Fight."

How bloodthirsty, when all Elspeth wanted was for the handsome stranger and this woman to have some respect for their partners. *Or, at the very least, if he must kiss someone, he could have kissed me.*

But, no. He'd chosen the woman swinging at her.

Annoying twat.

Elspeth caught the Jezebel's fist and held it. "You really shouldn't have done that."

"Or what?" snarled the other woman. She swung her other fist. Elspeth dodged it and then snapped one of her own out.

Crack. The woman dropped to the floor.

Damned humans and their soft heads.

A male voice from behind exclaimed, "Hey now, no fighting in my bar."

A meaty hand grabbed her by the arm, and Babsy yelled, "Don't you touch her, buddy." Then proceeded to jump on his back.

Given the bartender was at least a foot and a half taller than Babsy—in her human shape—she didn't quite manage to take him down.

The bartender whirled, which was kind of comical, given Babsy clung monkey-tight to him. Having ended up by her table again, Elspeth grabbed her glass and drained it.

Funny how the water warmed her belly. It didn't usually do that.

Someone tapped her on the shoulder, and she turned with a bright smile. "Yes?"

"You hit our friend." A gaggle of women with too much makeup confronted her.

"Your friend is a whore." Elspeth only told them what they probably already knew, and yet the supposed friends took offense. They rushed Elspeth, who giggled as she said, "Bar fight!" She already knew how this would end.

It didn't stop her from enjoying herself.

When one of the women lunged, she snared her and launched her over the counter. Then she lifted another and tossed her into a third. Exhilaration warmed her blood. *No wonder people like sparring.*

She wanted more. Elspeth looked around and clapped her hands. "Oh, come on, everyone. Don't be shy!"

When no one came to fight, she stalked over to the yelling bartender and punched him in the face.

He dropped, and Babsy leapt off before he crashed.

"Ah, man, did you have to do that? I was about to beat my bucking human record," Babsy pouted.

Crack. The sound of a bat getting slammed on the bartop drew attention. A new man had appeared behind the bar and pointed his bat. "Get the fuck out of my bar, you lunatics."

"A weapon isn't very sporting," Elspeth remarked. "Let me help you with that."

Leaning over, she snatched the weapon and brought it down over her upraised thigh. It didn't break, but it did bend.

She handed it back. "There you go. Now that you can't cheat, shall we dance?" She beckoned with her fingers. "Although, before we do, mind giving me another glass of that fancy water?"

"That wasn't entirely water," Babs muttered. "It might have had some vodka in it."

"You gave me alcohol." Elspeth's eyes widened. "Oh, dear. That explains a lot. You might want to clear the place."

"Why?"

"Because—" Elspeth might have said more except she caught a glimpse of *him*. He of the gorgeous blue eyes.

My eyes.

And the whore was back touching him. Clinging to his arm. Whining that she needed rescue.

"Get your hands off him!" Elspeth roared.

She blinked as she charged. The blood pumping hard. Her control slipping…

And found herself hanging over someone's back, the smell of smoke in her nostrils.

"Wh-wha-at h-h-appened?" she slurred.

"You destroyed the bar."

Shit. Not again. Mother would freak.

"What are you doing?"

"Carrying you."

"Put me down." She wouldn't want him to hurt himself.

"When I'm done with you. Go back to sleep." He snapped his fingers and whispered a word she didn't understand.

Zzzzz.

Chapter Seven

Alfred didn't say a word when Luc asked him to open the boot of the beastless carriage. Nor did he comment when Luc tossed his burden inside.

Alfred waited until they'd embarked on the route for home before clearing his throat and remarking, "Kidnapping is a felony."

"Is there anything that isn't a crime by human standards?" Luc grumbled because it seemed at every turn there was some kind of law against something. It really cramped his plans for world domination.

"Might I ask why you felt a need to kidnap Miss Elspeth?"

"The woman foiled my plans for coitus."

"Hence why you knocked her unconscious, abducted her, and set fire to the tavern."

"Me?" Luc couldn't help an indignant lilt. "I had nothing to do with the violence that erupted." Although he had greatly enjoyed it. Enough that, when Elspeth went a little crazy and began throwing chairs and laughing with great gusto when she knocked someone down, he'd stepped in just when a large fellow thought he could accost her.

"Don't touch her," he'd growled at the man in the bar. No one was to lay a hand on the dragoness. No one but him.

For revenge, of course.

Nothing else.

Now if only he could get his damned cock to forget how it felt to have her in his arms. Plush and womanly.

"Miss Elspeth was involved in a violent fracas?" Alfred shook his head as his query brought Luc back to the present. "I find that hard to believe."

Luc didn't. She was a big and bold warrior female, obviously. The kind his people used to produce before they became pacifists.

"Her friend helped with the chaos, too."

"Won't her friend notice that you kidnapped Miss Elspeth?"

"Her friend was the one to encourage me to take her." Which he found immediately suspicious since the other female was also a dragon.

However, given the humans running screaming from the burning building while Elspeth giggled, in between chugging from various bottles, he could see how the friend might have wanted a male to step in and take control.

So Luc had. Stepped close, that was.

"Cease your actions at once."

One eye closed, the other open and glazed, Elspeth smiled. Sloppily. "Make me, handsome."

Handsome? She found him attractive. How dare she try to

disarm her enemy with flattery. He didn't fall for it for a single moment.

Okay, maybe his cock did, but he knew she lied.

"You ruined my evening," he declared.

"You're a buzz kill," was her reply, followed by a belch that ignited. The fiery gas bubble floated away and clung to the ceiling, blackening a new spot.

"You don't hold your liquor well."

"Ma-ma-mother says I shouldn't drink."

Given the chaos, he could see why.

"You leave me no choice," he declared. "You wrecked my plans."

"Saved you, more like. How could you do that to Alfred?" she said with a wag of her finger. "You're supposed to be in loooooove."

"What are you speaking of, woman?" he asked, sidestepping when a human went screeching by screaming, "Fi-i-i-r-r-e."

Way to state the obvious.

"You and Alfred. And your relationship. How could you cheat on him like that?"

His mouth rounded, and he grabbed her by the arm to yank her close just as a section of the ceiling by the bar collapsed. "Are you implying I am amorously involved with Alfred?"

"Aren't you? I mean, you live together and all, and he calls you master."

"Because he is my manservant. He works for me."

"Works?" Her eyes widened with a temporary moment of lucidity. "So you're not screwing?"

"Most assuredly not!"

"Oh. Are you married?"

"No."

"Dating someone?"

"No."

"Then that means it's okay for me to do this." She leaned forward and kissed him.

Pressed her damned mouth to his, causing his senses to awaken all at once while sucking all the breath from his lungs.

He couldn't say anything, could merely enjoy the sensation of her mouth moving against his. The feel of her hands drawing him close. His own hands found their way around her body, the impression of her firm flesh even through her clothes exciting.

The squeeze of her against him, arousing.

He panted for air as she continued her embrace, siphoning his reasoning. Making him ignore the danger.

Danger? Smoke. Fire.

His eyes flashed opened as he realized something crucial.

The kiss was incredible.

No, not that. She was killing him, with pleasure! That was her plan.

And it worked. He'd never been harder or more aroused.

Completely unnatural and devious, which was why he pushed away from her.

Her eyes were soft, her lips parted and full. The color on them smudged. A wipe of his hand across his mouth showed a red streak. Her mark on him.

He wasn't sure how he felt about that. She reached for him—

Clonk. The falling light fixture knocked her out cold, sending her into a heap on the floor.

He regarded her for a moment, taking note of the fire all around that crept closer. He should walk out and let her burn.

Burn for the sins of her ancestors.

Burn for igniting his lust.

Burn for casting a spell on him that wouldn't let him walk away.

Perhaps his revenge would be better served by not letting her have a quick death.

Reaching down, he lifted her into his arms and transported her through the inferno, his lungs not bothered by the smoke. The heat barely kissing his exposed skin. His clothes, though, smoldered, and he noticed Elspeth turned a rosy shade of pink. Interesting. Her human form wasn't impervious to fire. Was her dragon?

Exiting outside, he heard sirens, screams. Even saw a flash as people held up tiny squares aimed in his direction.

Was he under attack? He bared his teeth and roared, and for a moment, his true self shimmered through. Only barely, but he felt some grim satisfaction in seeing the humans scatter with screams of "Monster!"

Not exactly. His kind preferred the term demon.

Elspeth chose that moment to wake, her query soft and vulnerable.

"Wh-wha-at h-h-appened?" she slurred.

"You destroyed the bar." In a most spectacular fashion.

"What are you doing?"

"Carrying you."

"That doesn't seem proper. I don't even know your name," she protested.

"I am Lucifer."

"Aha, knew you were a handsome devil." She giggled. "You really should put me down."

He held her closer. "When I'm done with you. Go back to sleep." He muttered a guttural word of power, a sleeping spell that worked even on dragons. One he could use now that he was free of the dungeon with the thick layers of magic that prevented it.

Her eyes shut. Her body went limp, and he slung her over his shoulder, ready to leave, only to have her short friend plant herself in front of him.

"Whatcha doing with Elsie?"

"Taking her to my lair and torturing her for answers."

The woman squinted at him. "You going to kill her?"

"Uh, no." Not initially. He had too many questions.

"How's your personal injury insurance?"

He frowned. "My what?"

"I don't suppose you'd sign an indemnity form?" the friend asked.

"A what?"

"I'm going to take it you don't keep a lawyer on retainer."

He drew himself tall, knowing enough about lawyers from the telly-vision to assert, "I am not a criminal."

"Good enough for me. Just remember to wear a rubber."

A statement that made absolutely no sense, and yet it proved enough to have the short friend trot off. Leaving him with Elspeth still draped over his shoulder.

A few more paces, and he was well away from the burning tavern and the approaching sirens.

Alfred was parked nearby, and that was how he ended up smelling of smoke, with a female dragon in his trunk, listening to Alfred lecture him about, "…might cause some trouble. What happened to simply finding a sexual partner?"

"I had one but *she*"—of the golden hair who smelled so much better than the woman who'd accosted him with her mouth—"interfered."

"Really? I wonder why."

Luc wasn't about to explain her erroneous assumption that he was involved with his manservant. "Because I told you, she is out to destroy me."

"Or she was jealous."

The very idea clamped his lips shut. Preposterous, of course. They'd met once. Briefly. More likely, she worried about him gathering human allies that would support him in his bid for world domination.

"What will you do with her?" Alfred asked.

Strip her naked and lick her like she once threatened to do to me.

"Lock her in the dungeon." He'd deal with her later, after a cold shower. A long one.

Chapter Eight

Babette had just gotten out of the shower when her phone rang. No avoiding it.

She answered. "Elspeth and Babette's legendary whore house. How may we blow you?"

"I want to speak with my daughter."

"Elsie can't come to the phone right now."

"Why not?"

She braced for the coming screech. "Because she's not here."

"What do you mean Elspeth isn't with you? You were supposed to look after her!" Elspeth's mother's voice rose in pitch.

"Listen, Auntie Klarice." Distant aunt, but the woman needed softening right now. A reminder she shouldn't kill Babette since they were related—if very, very distantly—was in order. "She went off with a man." A guy who was actually kind of interesting. Especially since he was the first person she'd ever heard of able to set Elsie off.

Usually, Elsie was the type to preach about turning

the other cheek. Forgiveness. And all kinds of other stupid bullshit.

Not tonight. Apparently, it only took a glass of liquid courage for Elspeth to embrace her dragon roots. To show herself capable of meting out destruction and throwing herself at a man.

Last Babette saw, Elsie had her mouth plastered to his. She didn't need to see anything after that. Bleached eyeballs hurt and did nothing to erase the memories. Babette knew this firsthand because she'd tried after catching Nana in the act.

As she was pouring the liquid into her eyes, Grandmother had claimed sex at her age was natural. Meanwhile, the sight of all that wrinkly flesh left Babette scarred for life.

"A man? What man? Dear God, I thought you were going to keep an eye on her. Do you know what happened to the last man she went off with?"

Everyone had heard. The shifter ended up in traction, babbling about how Elspeth had just about ripped off his dick.

Pussy. Wasn't Elsie's fault she had a lusty appetite in the bedroom.

"Don't worry, Auntie Klarice. This one seemed pretty sturdy."

"The one she put in the hospital three years ago was seven feet and three hundred pounds. He's still in rehab."

"Humans," she scoffed.

"He was a Kodiak bear shifter."

"Obviously, a runt."

"Does she at least have her medicine with her?"

"What meds?" Babette frowned. She'd not heard

anything about Elsie being sick. She wandered into the bathroom and noted a bulging makeup bag. She unzipped it and eyed the many bottles.

"Elspeth has certain—" Auntie Klarice paused. "—challenges when it comes to reality. The medicine helps her not get distracted."

It was also probably why she didn't drink. Zipping up the bag, Babette decided there was no need to let Auntie know about their visit to the bar. Elsie would be fine. "I'm sure she knows what she's doing." Maybe.

"Obviously not, or she wouldn't have gotten involved in that tavern fracas. And don't think we didn't hear about it. It's all over the news. We've got a tech cleaning crew trying to erase her part in it as we speak. I can't believe she was drinking. She knows how it affects her."

And now, so did Babette. It was awesome.

Odd how finding out that Elspeth wasn't always perfect increased her fondness for the girl.

"Elsie is fine. Nothing wrong with getting a little wild and blowing off some steam. Happens to all of us. I'll let you know if you have to cough up bail money. As for that guy she hooked up with, I don't think we need to worry. He's not human." Not by a long shot. As a matter of fact, he smelled downright exotic. If he had a sister, Babette would be all over her.

"Elspeth is a good girl, unlike some other people I know." Auntie's insinuation didn't insult.

Babette was well aware of her rightly earned reputation. "Don't worry. I'm working on her. By the time she comes home, she'll be new and improved."

"What's that supposed to mean?"

"We both know she missed out on the arrogance

gene." Poor thing was handicapped in that area. She even believed in sharing. Made a girl wonder exactly what Elspeth hoarded. Because every dragon had a hoard. Most tended toward a collection of items they thought precious—Babette was partial to tootsie rolls as a portable hoard, but she had a cousin who collected chocolate bar wrappers. Only one of each type. She travelled around the world to find them and kept them inside the set of the Willy Wonka factory that she'd had custom replicated inside a derelict building.

What did Elspeth treasure?

"Don't you dare mess with my girl!" Auntie yodeled. "You don't know what you're doing."

"Then why don't you come here since I'm so incompetent?" Babette snapped. "I'm doing my best. It's not as if Elsie came with warnings."

Auntie uttered a sigh, and her voice softened. "Sorry to yell. I'm just worried about her. You need to find her. Elspeth is naïve when it comes to people. Especially men. And she needs those pills."

"She's a big girl. She can take care of herself." Especially after a shot of vodka. That right hook had been impressive.

A growl vibrated the phone. "Don't make me crawl through this phone line and throttle you, Babette Silvergrace. I allowed the king to send Elspeth on this mission with you because I'd heard through the winevine"— because grapes were for humans—"that it was a nothing mission. Just those green heifers looking for attention on account of the king and his brother never having looked in their direction before choosing their mates."

"Actually, I think something is going on," Babette replied. While the missing dragons had supposedly returned, the humans hadn't. Not one. And of even more interest, all those taken were female. Young. Attractive. Petite females.

As a giant, Elspeth would be fine… Erm…maybe. "Um, I gotta go. Just remembered I have to, um, change my tampon."

"Find my daughter, or your mother will be looking for you at the bottom of the ocean," were Auntie's final words before she hung up.

Leaving Babette to wonder if perhaps she shouldn't have handed Elsie off to a stranger so quickly. The man did have an odd smell about him.

And he'd seemed rather miffed at Elsie cock-blocking him.

But they kissed.

Perhaps that was how he lured the women to his lair!

"Well, hot damn, Elsie," Babette muttered aloud. "And here I thought you were just being your annoying self, when all this time, you were laying a trap."

Brilliant. It kind of made Babette wish she'd thought of it, but then she might have had to kiss a man.

Blerg. She'd let Elsie do the dirty work. However, she'd have to locate her and swoop in just in time to reap the glory.

Elsie wouldn't mind because sharing was caring.

Chapter Nine

The dream began as it always did with the moment Luc realized his father was a coward.

"What are you doing?" barked Beelzebub at Asmoneus, his mate.

She whirled and hid Lucifer with her frame, not an easy feat given how gaunt she'd become—the once thickset woman now little more than skin and bones. "I'm doing nothing."

"Will you compound the matter with lies? Have we fallen so low?" Beelzebub asked.

His mother sneered, her lip curled high over her teeth, pride hinting through the grime and despair coating her skin. "We are held prisoner because of our own naivety. We cannot fall any lower."

"Remember our history lest we fall prey to the sins of our ancestors. Their lies and deceit led to—"

She interrupted. "Led to us being prisoners in our own dungeon." She swept a hand and gestured to the stone block walls, dark and cold. The barred door through which they received sparse sustenance.

"Unlike our ancestors, we remained firm in our beliefs."

"How can you not see it? We were cowards," his mother spat. "Our ancestors are turning over in their graves, ashamed of our cowardice. We should have fought."

Beelzebub folded his hands in his sleeves, a male who'd once appeared larger than life to a little boy. Now…Luc had nothing but disdain for the man who'd let his people down. And continued to betray them. "Violence is not the answer."

"Neither is starving. Or allowing ourselves to be taken without protest."

"By fighting, we are no better than the suzerain and her people."

"People! They are not people. They are dragon mages, ousted from their world for crimes against their kind. Criminals! And you allowed them free rein."

"They were banished like we were. Over time, I'd hoped they would adopt our ways."

"Yet, instead, they chose to study the forbidden texts and then used them against us. We gave them the keys to our destruction."

At the time, Luc didn't completely understand what his mother meant. But he did later on. Understood that the dark magic they'd harbored was ultimately their death knell.

"Perhaps we should have destroyed the ancient books."

"What we needed to do was fight," his mother exclaimed, pacing the cell, the tattered length of her robe swaying with every step. "By fighting, maybe we would have had a chance! Perhaps our son could have had a future."

"What do you want me to say?"

"You've said enough and done even less." Asmoneus held herself tall, her bearing regal despite the rags she wore. "You asked what I was doing. Giving my son, *our* son, my portion of food."

"Asmo, you mustn't. You'll starve." Father appeared stricken.

But his mother didn't care. Luc had never seen her so angry. "What if I do starve? What of it? I am old, Bez. My time in this world is almost done. His, though…" She cast a fond look at Luc, a youngling who'd yet to see any stubble on his jaw. "He might still have a chance if he can escape."

"Escape to where?" His father spread his hands. "There is nowhere to go on this plane where she won't find him."

"There are other worlds."

"We both know the suzerain has drained the life from all the portals. There is no escape."

His mother remained undaunted by Father's excuses. "For now. The alignment of the original world approaches."

"We are forbidden on that plane."

"I care not what people long dead decreed," his mother spat. "We are dying, Bez. How many of us are left?"

Too few at that point. They no longer had the numbers to fight even if they wanted to.

"Perhaps it is for the best."

The scary part was that his father truly believed they

deserved to die. Deserved to have the suzerain sweep in while they slept and imprison them all. Then slowly suck the life from each and every one of them until only a few were left.

She'd kept him and Father and Mother alive the longest. Voadicia needed the knowledge in his parents' heads because, despite centuries of learning, she knew there were still secrets to be discovered. But eventually, hunger won out.

The day she'd come for Father, Mother had tried to intervene. She'd beat on the corpulent guards with her fists, to no avail, while Father did nothing.

Beelzebub held out his hands to be shackled and said, "I go in peace. Fare thee well, my mate. Fare thee well, my son. We shall meet again if the fates decree it."

And then Father was gone, leaving Mother to sob and call him a fool. Leaving a young man to wonder how long before he was next.

It was a while… The suzerain was determined to stretch her last meals. But, eventually, they came for his mother.

She didn't go quietly. She cursed and kicked and screamed. Despite having never transformed because of their laws, in a fit of desperation, she managed to let the beast out.

The horns on her forehead emerged, stubby and black. Her teeth turned razor-sharp. The mighty wings at her back unfurled as she attacked.

She took the guards by surprise, especially since she was the first of their kind to finally fight back. To say "no!" to fate.

Lucifer ran to aid his mother, his fists pummeling at the guards' thick girth.

One of them, Maedoc, grabbed Luc then lifted him and held him in front of his mother, a knife at his neck. "Enough," he said softly. "Don't make me kill the boy."

Mother stilled. Her black lips peeled back to bare her teeth as she hissed, "Don't you dare hurt him."

"If you want to save him, then you will come with us quietly."

"Why? So you can kill him tomorrow or the next day?" She sneered, a mighty expression full of disdain. "Perhaps it would be best if you killed him now rather than allow Voadicia to suck him dry."

"You would really stand by and watch as he bleeds?" The tip of the knife pricked, and yet Luc wasn't afraid. Death was but a new beginning.

"Don't hurt him." Mother shrank back into herself, naked and dirty, her body thin, every bony nuance showing through the skin.

"What will you give us if we shield your son from harm?"

"Anything."

"Anything?" Maedoc leaned forward and whispered something to her. She blanched but nodded. Maedoc demanded, "Swear by the magic."

Luc hadn't understood at the time; only later did he realize the bargain she'd made.

She hugged him one last time and whispered words that he barely understood through his grief. But later, replayed.

Mother placed her arms behind her back as they tethered her in chains. She held his gaze and said, "You must be brave, Lucifer. Remember what I said."

He remembered. How could he forget?

"You are the last of our branch. You are descended

from the original Shining One. The only remaining heir to the King of Fierce Countenance. It is up to you to carry on the family name. But not the new traditions. Not this perversion of who we've become." His mother whispered the words his father would have called treason. "I call upon you to avenge our people. To throw off the shackles that bind us. To spill the blood of our enemies and regain control of our world."

What world?

Once his mother had left, it was just him. For years. Because Voadicia forgot he existed, or perhaps his jailors had lied. It didn't matter. Luc survived alone in that cell for a long time. Subsisting on the water that eked out from a crack in the foundation. By feasting on the flesh of the rodents that had escaped the fate of everything else.

In solitude, he exercised to become strong. Practiced the magic his mother had taught him in secret. Sometimes, even exchanging that knowledge for outside treats when his captors made their rare visits.

He'd fully expected to die in that cell, failing to keep the promise he'd made to his mother. The magic keeping him bound within those walls was stronger than one demon alone could fight.

The failure burned bitter like the acid the rodents spat when he stepped on their tails before wringing their necks. What also burned was the fact that he owed his freedom to Maedoc and Eogan. The pair who'd kept him alive, had also set him free in the end.

When the door swung open, at first, he'd thought it a jest. A trick, surely.

Yet when they didn't return, Luc stepped out of his

cell. A prison he'd lived in since not long after his conception. He might have rejoiced, except what was there to celebrate?

The mighty castle loomed dark and silent around him. Dusty. Empty. A ghost of what it once was.

He exited the citadel, his step jaunty and excited, only to stagger to a stop as he stared.

The world his mother had described loomed dead all around. The trees but barren husks. The ground dusty. Not a speck of color to be seen. The lushness of their world killed by the dragons that had siphoned every ounce of life from the land.

Luc had never had the chance to see true living color. He'd had to rely on pictures in books. On the vivid recollections of the old ones—who became the first victims to feed Voadicia and her insatiable hunger.

Father was right. There is nothing for me here.

Maedoc and Eogan had freed him to rule over a wasteland. All that remained was the bitter taste and smell of defeat.

But it didn't have to be the end. Luc didn't have to be his father and go meekly to his fate. He wanted to be like his mother and fight.

With that goal in mind, despite his inexperience, he followed the tracks of the ones who'd set him free. Followed them to an ancient portal created by those who'd lived in Hell before his people. Large stone arches engraved and tingling with ancient magic. Doorways to other dimensions.

He wasn't sure he could activate the doorway. It probably involved some intricate ceremony or fancy words.

I can't escape.

The defeatism in that sentiment froze him. Would he truly walk away without trying? Let doubt guide his hand?

All his life, he'd waited for a chance, an opportunity to do something. That chance had arrived.

If the dragons could use the portals, then surely he could, as well.

Placing his hand on the stone dais, the cool flow of magic surprised him. He'd not done anything to activate it, and yet the portal reacted, coming alive and powering up.

He snatched his hand away and stared.

The archway turned dark then lightened to become a misty gray. The doorway to a new future. The catch? Once he stepped through…there was no guarantee he could return.

I should wait. Explore. Find supplies. Books. All things that would take time. He stared at the oddly opaque surface of the portal. A doorway out of here.

What if he delayed and the door shut? What if the alignment of the worlds changed? What if he missed his chance?

Then I die here. Alone. Last of my kind. Perhaps that was for the best.

That was a thought Father would have. He aspired to being more like his mother. Shoulders back. Show no fear.

Inhaling deeply, he took a last look at his world.

His dead world.

He wouldn't dishonor his mother and his ancestors by staying here to die, too.

It's up to me now to rebuild what was lost.

It wasn't fear that coursed through his veins as he took the needed steps through the portal, but anticipation.

Finally, he was doing something other than merely surviving.

He was—

Dying!

Lucifer choked as he emerged through the portal into a new land and breathed fresh air for the first time.

The sweetness brought tears to his eyes. The purity dropped him to his knees with weakness. He bowed his head as he finally understood exactly what had been taken from him.

Everything.

Standing on the parapet of the crumbling castle that his ancestors had once owned, he surveyed the land he'd come to. Lush. Green. Alive…

Mine. The dragons had taken everything in his world. It seemed only fair that he return the favor.

Soon, you will know my name. You will fear it.

My name is Lucifer, the last of the Shining Ones. And this world is about to become mine.

Mine.

Mine.

The word chanted itself over and over and—

Someone replied!

"Considering we barely know each other, declaring I'm yours seems a bit premature, but what the heck. You can be mine, too."

His eyes shot open as his vivid dream—a replay of the past—shattered, and he beheld the woman atop him.

A woman in his room. "How did you escape your

cell?" he barked. Because he'd locked the dragon with the yellow curls away himself. Then asked Alfred to find a chain so that he might also tether the bars to prevent her escape should she know how to use the magic box with the symbols on it.

Her lips curved. "Alfred let me out."

The traitor.

"And you came to kill me?" he snarled.

"Not exactly. Is this your way of saying I am squishing you?" She looked chagrinned and bit her lower lip. She adjusted her weight, in that she lifted herself from his body and went to move away.

But he liked her weight atop him.

His hands shot out from under the blankets and tethered themselves to her waist. "Where are you going?"

"You said I was killing you. I didn't mean to crush you. Then again, you'd think I'd know by now that I'm not exactly dainty. But you were thrashing in your sleep, and I was worried you were having some kind of a fit, which is why I hopped on top—"

"You're not heavy."

The simple truth halted her flood of words and brought a bright smile to her face. It also brought a massive erection. Surely, the blanket would hide its presence.

"I'm glad you're awake." She squirmed atop him, exacerbating his turgid state. "I wanted to thank you for taking care of me during my little mishap in the bar."

"You destroyed the place." He'd found it rather fascinating that such a beautiful woman could mete out violence while smiling.

"Yeah." Her cheeks pinked. "I am sorry about that. I don't hold my alcohol very well."

"Then why drink?"

"I don't. Usually. My bestie played a prank."

"Her prank burned down a tavern, caused injury, and resulted in me failing in my mission to acquire coitus." Although, he failed to mention that, other than the lack of sex, he'd rather enjoyed the other parts.

"About that… You really shouldn't go around having sex with strangers."

"I knew her name." Kind of. Beth. Or was it Meth? She'd said something along those lines.

"Which reminds me, we were never properly introduced. I'm Elspeth, but the king calls me Elsie." She sat up straighter on him, applying pressure to his groin as she held out a hand.

He sucked in a breath. Had she done it on purpose? "I don't care about your name."

"Is it because you don't want to have sex with me?" Her smile faded for a moment. "That's okay. I have a reputation, so it's probably for the best."

"A reputation for what?"

"Being a little rough."

"And the problem with that is?"

The brilliance of her smile returned, blinding him. "I wish more men had your attitude and were tough like you." She bounced, and this time, he did groan. "Oh, dear. Did that hurt?"

Was it possible to hurt in a good way? Obviously, the answer was yes, given he'd like her to bounce some more. But he needed to look past the enjoyment to her true purpose.

Don't forget what she is.

"Why are you here?" Other than for the obvious: torture.

"Well, I couldn't exactly leave without saying thank you."

"Who said you could leave? Return to your cell at once. You are supposed to be my prisoner."

"Return to that icky stable?" Her nose wrinkled. "But your bed is so much more comfortable. Can't you hold me prisoner here?"

She flopped beside him. Then wormed under the covers.

"This behavior is unseemly." Even he knew that.

"Is this because you haven't introduced yourself yet? Because I keep waiting for you to say, 'hi, my name is…'" she prompted.

"My name is none of your business."

"Do you prefer me to use None when addressing you? Or Business?"

"Are you for real?"

"I get asked that a lot, which is weird because I don't think I look fake. Do I feel fake?" Under the covers, she grabbed his hand and tugged it over to rest just above her breast.

If he slid it down just a little, he could cup it. What would she say if he removed her shirt and kissed it? And…

What am I thinking? She's a dragon.

His cock didn't care. He throbbed. Every inch of him ached. Even his gums.

What was wrong with him?

Or maybe it wasn't him. Maybe it was her. She must

be poisoning him somehow with irrational logic and desire.

Now to figure out why he liked it. He leaned toward her. She didn't recoil.

"Why are you really here?"

"I thought I was here to say goodbye, but now I realize that perhaps I should just stick around on account of the view being quite nice." She stared at his face as she wound herself around him.

He preferred her on top. So he put her there, grabbing her around the waist and tugging her back where she belonged.

"Stay." A command and plea in one.

"It would be rude for me to run off." She gave a grind of her hips against his, a sensual and sexual thing.

"Manners are important." Their eyes locked as their lower bodies moved. Subtle pressure. A tingling enjoyment.

She dipped lower, her lips barely brushing his. Stealing his breath.

Stealing my soul!

Get away! Luc rolled out of the bed and stood alongside it, confronting her.

"You tried to kill me!"

On hands and knees, she pursed her lips. "I resent that. You are perfectly intact. No broken bones. Obviously conscious, as well."

"Only because I saw through your plan."

"My plan to cock-block myself." For a moment, her lips turned down then, as if jolted, they slammed up into a smile. "Good thing I've got a fresh pack of batteries at home."

He didn't know what batteries did, or what cock-blocking had to do with it, but he did know one thing.

"Your gown. It's quite splendid."

"Thank you." She peeked down at her dress. "Custom-made because I don't have a common figure."

"I could use a good tailor."

"I'll dig up his number."

As he opened his mouth to say thank you, he realized what she'd done.

She'd lowered his defenses with her pleasant demeanor. She'd removed his common sense with her physical body. Her womanly attire with its shockingly short hem seemed much more attractive to him than those in the form-fitting tights they mockingly called pants.

"Stop what you're doing."

"What am I doing?" She blinked long lashes at him.

He almost reached out to tug her close. He flattened his lips instead. "It won't work. I know what you are. What you plan." He stood tall as he confronted her.

"I guess I'm not very subtle about it. I just can't hide my fascination with you. And it's unseemly. A male obviously prefers to chase the woman. Not vice versa. But it's your fault for being so intriguing. Did you know you're in my dreams?"

She dreamt of him? Almost, she caught him in her spell. He shook it off. "You can't confuse me with your words."

"I don't suppose you can translate them for me? Because even I get lost. Sometimes, I wonder if I'm trying to sabotage the ending."

The statement made little sense. "What ending?"

"The happy one."

"Happiness is but a myth." That might have been spoken with a touch of cynicism.

"Happiness is sometimes hard to find; however, it does exist."

"Not for me." The words slipped out. He clamped his lips tight.

"You still have a chance. To be happy."

"You're right. I almost did. Last night, until you interrupted."

He noticed her eyes glow, turning almost milky, as she growled, "That was necessary for a happy ending."

"So you claim, and yet I am the one left unsatisfied." A bold claim, and yet something about her frankness called him to speak openly.

"I'd satisfy."

He kept his hands over his erection in hopes that she wouldn't notice. "You wish to bed me?"

"More than you can imagine. However, I should warn you. I've been known to get a little rough when enthusiastic."

His nostrils flared. "You've touched others?" For some reason, the very idea offended him.

"I'm not as innocent as I look."

She didn't look innocent at all. The dress she wore molded to her upper body, outlining her womanly shape. She had left the bed to stand in front of him, close enough that the fabric of her skirt touched his sleep bottoms. A few inches taller than her meant his dropped gaze was perfectly aligned with hers.

Her lips a mere breath away.

I could kiss her. He shouldn't. What of his revenge? His promise?

She's the enemy.

She was touching. Igniting him. His passion flared, and when she pulled away, he almost roared in loss. Almost yelled at her to return. He wasn't done.

His eyes blazed as he huffed hotly.

Elspeth stroked fingers down his face. "Holy smoking brisket barbecued with sauce, you have horns!"

Chapter Ten

"No, I don't."

What an odd thing to deny. She cocked her head and squinted, but the horns remained. "Yeah, you do. Itty bitty ones trying to poke out of your forehead."

His hand rose to rub across the expanse, and he frowned. "This is your fault."

"Are your horns an allergic reaction to me?"

"They're a reaction, all right," he grumbled.

"Perhaps we should see a doctor and have something prescribed for your allergy." Or not. The tiny nubs gave him a dashing air.

"How about you leave instead of vexing me to the point where I lose control?"

She frowned. "But a moment ago, you told me to get back to my stall in the barn. You really should make up your mind."

"Are all dragons as annoyingly obtuse as you."

"Actually, I'm the nice one. Most of my kin aren't as accommodating. I'm considered handicapped because I don't have the proper amount of arrogance." Or a hoard that they knew about. "I can't help it if I prefer to be happy and helpful."

"Dragons are vile and heartless creatures. I can see how that would irritate them."

His agreement wasn't exactly a positive thing. Yet, on the plus side, he was talking to her. "How come you hate dragons so much?"

"Because they killed my people. And kept me prisoner for my entire life."

"You escaped, though."

"Only recently, and by accident. And they didn't do me a kindness. The dimension they freed me into was a dead place. If I'd not escaped via a portal, I'd have died."

"Wait a second." The gears in her mind turned as she put the pieces together. "You're from the same place as that crazy lady we fought in the grand battle. The one with the red eyes."

"Voadicia, who styled herself suzerain in my world." He sneered. "Because of her, I had to leave."

"What did she do?" Because she'd only heard bits and pieces.

"Are you going to tell me you don't know of her crimes?"

"We don't exactly get your news channel. I know that, while she was here, she meddled in our politics." And there were other rumors of her taking over people's identities.

"That was how it started in our world, too. She arrived, centuries before, with the other dragon mages. Cast from this world because of a mistake," he said.

"If by mistake, you mean that those mages supposedly used their magic to overthrow the dragon monarchy. Only it ended up being a bad plan because the humans betrayed the mages and almost wiped us out."

"A pity they failed," he said with a sneer. "My ancestors also lacked the balls to do what needed to be done. Bloody pacifists who thought they could live in harmony with the dragon mages."

"Obviously, it wasn't too bad. You said this happened hundreds of years ago."

"Because that was how long it took her before she ran out of the living energy she needed to prolong her life and turned to her hosts instead."

"What living energy? I don't understand."

"No one did at first." His eyes took on a dreamy cast as he remembered aloud. "According to the elders who passed on the stories, Voadicia discovered the spell to prolong her life in an ancient text."

"A spell to live forever?" Her eyes widened. "Cool."

"Not really. Magic has a cost. Especially strong magic. The spell requires a certain perversion to happen. A theft, really. To prolong her life, she needed to take life. To siphon the essence of living things."

"Are you saying Voadicia was like a vampire?" She wrinkled her nose. While not exactly everyone's cup of tea, Elspeth didn't see the problem. People donated blood every day. What did it matter if it was for eating or transfusing?

"Vampire?" He frowned at her. "Do you speak of the mythical creatures I've seen within the moving picture frame? Alfred says they are not real."

"Apparently, they are." She rolled her eyes. "Like, duh, you just said Voadicia was sucking the life out of stuff."

"Living essence, not blood. Had it only been their

plasma, my world might have survived. But she needed their life force. Living things only have a certain amount to give before they die."

Elsie's lips pursed. "Didn't anyone notice her killing stuff?"

"Not at first. You see, she used the portals to visit other dimensions. Places without a dominant intelligent species. Away from prying eyes, she and her minions sucked the life out of everything they could, starting with the animals. Then the plants. She drained entire dimensions, leaving them barren. When those became useless to her, she turned to my land. And, eventually, my people."

"How many survived?"

"None."

The dark despair in his words managed to penetrate her usually happy bubble. It didn't help that she'd missed her daily dose of medicine. Her lips turned down. "She killed your family?"

He nodded. "Siphoned their lives to extend her own. I had to watch as my people were taken, one by one, to feed her hunger. To see the cells around me emptied until only my family remained. And then it was my parents' turn. Once they were snatched, I found myself alone."

Her lower lip trembled. Her eyes brimmed with tears. She couldn't find anything positive to say. Nothing. At. All.

It was so… "Horrible. How horrible!" she wailed. "OhmygodIamsosorry." She blubbered in a stream of words. "No wonder you hate dragons. We're awful. Wicked. Murderers. Oh, no." She sobbed. And sobbed.

"Stop that," he barked. "No crying."

"I can't. You're all alone in the world." The very idea broke her heart, and she wailed louder.

She also lunged and grabbed him into a hug, squeezing him tightly, and while nothing cracked, he did gasp.

"Unhand me."

"I can't. You need love. Even if…if you don't want it from me because I'm a horrible dragon." How could he stand to be close to her? She probably reminded him of his poor, dead parents.

The fire engine wail rose and fell with every heaving breath she took.

A crashing sound barely managed to penetrate her grief.

But she couldn't ignore Babsy yelling, "What the fuck is going on?"

Elsie raised her tear-stained face to see her bestie stomping into the bedroom, fists raised and clenched. A petite bundle of ire.

Any other time, she would have given her a hug, but instead, she blubbered, "Lucifer hates dragons."

For a moment, Babsy appeared puzzled, but then her gaze landed on Lucifer, and she snapped, "What the fuck did you do to her, asshole?"

He straightened. Trying to look stoic when, really, he was just all broken inside.

Elspeth blubbered anew. "Poor baby."

He glared at Elsie. "I am not a baby." Then a heated gaze directed at Babette. "And I did nothing. Yet she is carrying on as if… I don't know why she is acting thus. She is not the aggrieved one here."

"You must have done something," snapped Babsy,

dropping onto the bed beside Elspeth. She couldn't stop sobbing, even though Babsy patted her back.

"It's so sad," she hiccupped to Babette. "They're all gone."

"Who's all gone?"

"His family, and it's my fault."

Babsy sighed. "What the fuck did you do now, Elsie? Did you hug someone without asking first again? What have we said about running up to strangers? Remember Allentown?"

"I merely wanted to help the woman with her children and groceries."

"Snatching people's babies and tossing them into the air to stop them from crying isn't something you can do with humans."

"But it worked."

"And got you a citation. Now, you going to explain how you killed his family?" Babsy shot him a look. "I'll put a call in to the family lawyers, and we'll garner you some kind of compensation."

Luc recoiled as he pivoted, drawing attention to his body. He was a distracting hunk in low-hanging track pants that exposed his bulky body. Bulked with muscle, the dark tattoos on his flesh enhancing his perfection.

Elspeth ogled his half-naked frame, only belatedly realizing that if she could see his perfection, then so could Babs.

At least her bestie knew better than to stare at his impeccable pecs. She'd hate to take out her eyes. They were pretty.

"First of all, I never said she killed my family. She started that. And then she cried. I hate crying," said with a pointed look in Elspeth's direction.

"See. Luc hates me," she mumbled sadly. Which made her arousal and body tingling every time she saw him all the more wrong.

"I don't hate you," he snapped. "I hate dragons."

Babsy cocked her head. "Fair enough. I'd hate you, too, but that would imply caring what you thought, and you know what? I just really don't."

"But we should care because it is our fault. We sent the dragon mage to his dimension, and she ate his whole family, leaving him all—all-all alone." Elspeth wailed anew as the tragedy of it hit her.

Babsy gave her one last back rub before she jumped to her feet and stalked over to Luc. "What is wrong with you?" She jabbed him in the chest. A bare chest.

Skin to skin.

Elsie's tears stopped as heat suffused her, evaporating them.

She really shouldn't poke him like that.

"What's wrong with me?" He sounded rather incredulous. "How about the fact that your kind decimated my entire world?"

"The dragon mages did. Not us. And most definitely not her." Babs pointed her finger at Elsie. "She doesn't need a whining asshat telling her she's at fault when his damned people might have survived had they been impossibly better than dragons."

"Are you blaming us for their actions?"

"You tell me. Are you at fault?"

Elsie roused herself enough to exclaim, "Babsy, you can't blame the victim."

"Why the hell not? He thinks it's okay to unload on you. Casting the blame for his people's weakness on you. What is wrong with you?" Babette swung her glare onto him. "Can't you fucking tell she's sensitive?" Babsy yelled at Lucifer, and he got that look on his face again.

Elspeth struggled to her feet, tangled somehow in the sheets, and staggered toward them. "Don't yell at him, Babsy. It's not his fault." She stood in front of him. "He needed to express his feelings. How can he heal without expelling his anger?"

"Now he needs to damned well apologize, or he'll be healing from my fist." Babette leaned around to shake one in his direction.

"In the dungeon, I learned to eat any kind of flesh. I have to say, since arriving here, I've been wondering about the taste of dragon."

"Did you just threaten to eat me?" Babsy wrinkled her nose. "Dude, that is gross. I'm into chicks, not dicks."

He looked puzzled, whereas Elsie was a tad bit… angry? Which didn't make much sense. Why be upset? Look at them all talking. Without blood. Or hitting.

It wouldn't be hard to start the hitting. Starting with Luc, who really needs to put a shirt on. Really, flaunting himself like that. He's even tempting Babette.

Luc recoiled. "You flatter yourself if you think I would ever find a dragon attractive. To me, you are the enemy."

"We're not your problem, dude. Sounds like your issue is with Voadicia."

"My problem is with dragons," he pointed out.

"She was a dragon *mage*," Babsy corrected. "And we obviously understood she was badass, which was why she got exiled out of this world."

"You sent them to my world instead of executing them."

"Because, back then, they were related to people who didn't want to see them all die."

"You could have imprisoned them."

"We did. And then someone considered it mean, and so banishment was sought."

"Well, because your ancestors were soft, Voadicia and her cohorts continued to perpetrate their evil." He glared.

Elspeth sobbed. "You're right. We did it."

Babette barked, "Gawd's sake, Elsie. This is not our fault. Our ancestors tossed them into that hell world figuring they'd die out."

"Except Voadicia found a spell to extend her life at the expense of others."

"And whose fault is that?" Babsy rose on tiptoe and said much too nicely, "You guys were the ones who left that kind of magic lying around. Making you twat waffles. So, your fault."

His brows rose. "You would blame the eradication of my kind on me? Only a dragon would be so arrogant. Which is why your kind needs to die. I'm here to avenge my people."

"You and what army?"

"I don't need an army."

"Think you can take me? Bring it." Babette beckoned with her fingers.

Perhaps it was time for an intervention. Elspeth threw her arms around them both as best she could. "Make love, not war." She'd gladly donate her body to making love…to him. Babsy could watch since she didn't like boys. Sounded like a good plan all around.

She squeezed him tightly. He stiffened.

"What is she doing?" he whispered.

"Hugging," Babette said with a long sigh. "Which is better than the crying, so shut up and enjoy it."

"What if I don't want to enjoy it?"

"No one enjoys it, but given her special needs, we endure it."

"I can hear you," Elspeth replied. "And am so happy to see you starting to talk and become friends. It wouldn't do at all for my two besties to hate each other."

"Besties? What is she saying?" he asked.

Rather than let Babsy reply, Elspeth beamed at Lucifer. "You are no longer alone. I will make sure of that. Best friend."

Chapter Eleven

There were many ways Luc could have handled Elsie's proclamation.

Acceptance—which would have gone against all his plans for vengeance.

Murder—which, for some reason, he found himself reluctant to do.

Or the option he chose, getting rid of both Elsie and her irritating companion.

"Out." He broke free of the hug—and immediately missed the warmth. "Get out. Both of you, right now."

The cap of blonde curls swayed as Elsie shook her head. "I can't go now. We need to bond."

"We are not bonding. We are enemies."

"Not anymore. I'm going to do my best to make up for my naughty ancestors."

"How can you atone? You can't bring back the dead." He was blunt in his statement, and her lower lip trembled instantly, making him feel chagrined.

A Shining One feeling chagrined? That was his

father. He still had his balls. He straightened. "I want nothing but to see you dead."

"I'm sorry you're so broken. Just know that I've seen a few futures where you fare well." Her eyes welled with tears, and he looked away.

She wouldn't fell him with her false sympathy again. He didn't want pity. "Leave, and don't come back. Next time, I will act."

Kill her?

He couldn't. But he wanted her to believe he would. *She makes me feel weak.* Was there perhaps some truth to her earlier query about him having a reaction to her presence?

Perhaps there was a reason dragons and demons did not get along. Allergies.

"If you need me. Just call." She kept trying, but he didn't reply.

The one called Babsy snared Elsie by the arm and dragged her toward the door. "You heard the man. We should go. Like now. Later, dude."

"There will be no later!" he called after them, his feet rooted in place as the door slammed shut.

He remained frozen, somewhat bemused by the whole encounter.

Usually, when he woke from a dream, he was alone and angry. Then the anger at fate would curl into despair. Why did he continue to suffer? Why keep trying?

Dancing green eyes came to mind.

The woman plagued him something fierce. Even when she wasn't around.

He heard the purr of a motor, the glass in the windows not completely muffling it. She was gone.

Luc could relax. He still didn't move. How could he when he caught sight of the bed?

The remembered weight of her atop him enough to get him hard.

He'd yet to solve his coitus problem. He looked down at his groin and his hand. That method had always worked before, yet now, he found himself reluctant. She had, after all, expressed interest in him.

And I rebuffed her.

Which was truly the right thing to do. However, tell his cock that.

A brisk knock saw him diving under the covers, lest Alfred notice his turgid issue bulging the front of his loose pants.

He had to say he really enjoyed cotton. There was something quite liberating about how he could let it all hang loose inside the soft, roomy fabric.

There were plenty of things to like about this world. Including the ease of it. Taking over the castle had proven effortless. Almost too simple. The lords of this time having barely any security. No guards. No traps.

He'd more or less waltzed in and declared that he was the ruler. He ordered everyone into the stable dungeon. Only a few tried to run. Those proved fun to chase down.

His first successful coup.

Eventually, an heir might show to try and take the castle from Luc. If they did, he'd fight them. He'd been practicing. The moving picture frame taught him quite a bit about battle and strategy.

A knock and a questioning "Sir?" had him shouting, "Come in."

The door swung open. No clicking of a key first. He wasn't a prisoner here.

Never again.

Alfred appeared, pushing a cart on wheels. The metal and wood of it were sturdy, three shelves in total. The top one held three silver domes and a carafe of orange fluid.

Alfred wheeled it to the table flanked by seats that tried to swallow a man if he used them.

"You set the girl free." Luc stated it boldly and waited to see if Alfred would refute.

"I did." Alfred parked the cart.

"Permission wasn't given for that."

"One does not lock up our lady friends."

"She's not a lady." Which, he actually liked. "And we're not friends." Even if she'd tried to be.

"Is this your way of saying you killed her?"

The very idea startled Luc. "Do you see blood?"

"Not all deaths are messy. If you didn't kill her, then where is Miss Elspeth?"

"She left. With her friend." Who, while attractive, didn't draw him as much as the statuesque, curly-haired Elsie.

"Left? Seems rather abrupt. She was here but a moment. Did you frighten her off?"

Luc stiffened at the tone in his manservant's query. "What if I did? She is my enemy."

"Yes, I could see how dangerous she was." Spoken dryly.

It prickled Luc's pride. "There were two of them." When Alfred said nothing, he specified. "They're dragons. I can't consort with them."

"I didn't expect prejudice from you."

"It isn't prejudice. We are mortal enemies."

"Why?" Alfred asked, removing the domes on the cart with flair.

Luc approached, almost drooling at the sight of the waffles, a word he'd learned quickly after the first one he ate. Fluffy baked goodness. Whipped cream. Fruit. He loved juicy, flavorful fruit. And bacon.

A plateful of salt and another of sugar. He was in culinary heaven.

He sat down and spread a napkin across his lap. "Dragons killed my people."

"Those two girls didn't."

"But they are related"—even if distantly—"to those who did."

"Am I to understand that you want to punish them for the sins of their forefathers and mothers?"

"Yes."

"Did you hear the crazy in that statement, sir?"

"You would have me be like my father?" Luc sneered. "Weak. Afraid to fight. I won't be made a prisoner again by the dragons. They must pay for their sins."

"Let's say you do kill all the dragons. What then?" Alfred poured the juice and then lifted the lid on another dome, showing off some fluffy eggs and potatoes. Ambrosia for his palate.

"When the world is rid of dragons, I will be at peace." He sank into his first bite with closed eyes and a happy hum. Alfred wouldn't let it rest, though, and ruined his sugar buzz.

"Will you be at peace? I don't see how. Your family will still be gone. As will the only person to have extended a hand in friendship."

"She isn't my friend. You have let yourself be fooled. The dragoness offers a false hand. Her friend was more forthright. Even then, I will not be lulled into trusting that they might decipher my secrets."

"What secrets?" Alfred asked, whipping out the second plate of bacon from the other dome, which had more waffles.

He took those, too.

In between bites, he confided. "My plan to rule the world."

"Which isn't that big of a secret, as you keep telling everyone about it. Might I ask how you intend to achieve such a feat?"

"I'm still working on it."

Alfred refilled his juice glass. "Shouldn't you have an army if you wish to perform a coup?"

The dilemma of the last male of a race…how did he convince people to follow him?

"I've only just arrived. Once word goes out about the perfidy of dragons, and my presence is revealed, legions will flock to fight."

"What makes you think people will want to fight for you?"

"Because they'll want to free themselves from the dragon's yoke." He couldn't help a note of disdain.

"Except the dragons don't control anyone but the dragons. Humans rule themselves. What makes you think they want you to rule over them?"

"Because." He frowned at Alfred. "Shouldn't you be on my side?" Was his servant working against him, too?

"I am on your side, which is why I am pointing out the flaws in your logic. Did it ever occur to you that perhaps your vendetta is best left behind? You're here on earth now, sir, with a chance to start over."

"But my people…my promise…" An assurance made to his mother to make the dragons pay. Except, really, it was only one dragon and her two sycophants who were truly to blame.

Where was Voadicia? Elsie and her friend had mentioned her, and a battle. Had they killed the dragon mage? That would be a shame, given he'd dreamt of the many ways he'd flay her skin from her body then feast on her heart.

With a dash of Montreal steak spice to liven up the raw flesh. Alfred now had standing orders to feed him the best filet mignon, tartare style, once a week.

"The suzerain is gone?" Luc asked.

"Who is that?"

"Dragon mage. Although she probably no longer looked like one given the way she'd perverted her nature. She would have been a fearsome foe."

"There was something on the television. A bunch of amateur video footage showing dragons fighting. Big and small. All the colors of the rainbow."

Dragons fighting amongst themselves? Fascinating.

"Did many of them die?"

"I don't know." Alfred hid the cleared plates under the domes. "There was much effort made to hide the event."

"Did you see the suzerain, though?"

Alfred shrugged. "No idea. You'd have to find some footage. If the master likes, we can ask Google."

"Is he a seer? Does he see into the past?"

"In a sense. Think of it as an all-knowing servant."

"I wish to see this Google. And moving pictures for

this battle." He wanted to see for himself if the suzerain were truly gone. If not, he'd have to seek her out.

What if she was gone, though?

What then?

Her soldiers. Those obese beasts who did her every bidding. They'd set him free, but what happened to them?

He'd tried asking Alfred, but he didn't know much about the dragons or pertinent events.

But you do know someone who might be willing to tell you more about Voadicia.

"Alfred, I need you to fetch Elspeth."

"Exactly how am I to accomplish that?"

"By leaving this house and getting her." Seemed rather obvious. "I need to speak to her."

"If you want to talk, then call her."

"On the telephone?" He didn't trust those small rectangles of metal and glass with voices coming out of them.

"Yes, the phone. Did you get her number?"

Luc stared.

"Did you make plans to see her again at all?"

"Why would I meet with my enemy? I told her to get out. But I have changed my mind. I want her back."

"But have no idea where she is?" Alfred shook his head and sighed. "I'll do my best to find her, sir."

Find her and keep her. He almost didn't recognize the cold voice within as his own. But he knew what it meant.

My demon is rousing.

And Elspeth had claimed to see it.

When Alfred left, Luc finally made his way to the bathroom and its mirror for a look at his face.

His forehead especially. It appeared smooth.

Unblemished. Which he knew already from repeatedly running his hand over it; yet he'd hoped for more.

He grimaced. How foolish to hope he'd see a sign of the horns Elsie had supposedly seen.

She lied!

Thing was, he believed her. It was what his people used to be.

Demons. Swarthy skinned. The texture rougher, more protective. Winged, mighty spans capable of soaring flight. And horns. The larger, the more powerful you were in the demon magic.

But with that other powerful self came the pride and, most especially, the violence. Demons killed. Supposedly without care.

He wouldn't know. The world was their prison, the rocks in that place, especially the stone in the castles, rampant with a metal that made it impossible for them to change. That same rock ran in veins through their continent. It made it easy to change their ways.

They stopped transforming.

But worse than that. They didn't care. They were perfectly peaceful. They didn't need to be demons.

They didn't fight. Not even to save themselves.

I am not those who left before me…

Luc had a chance to do things differently. To fight for his freedom.

You're already free.

For now. What of when the dragons noticed and tried to imprison him? They were, after all, partially responsible for the demons being imprisoned in the first place. Letting them take some of the blame for the humans that kept disappearing. And then killing them off when they joined them in Hell, using them to further their own agenda.

I won't let that happen. He'd fight.

I might not have science, but I have magic. He reached out to tickle the edge of the magical river. Enough power to do what he needed. He gathered the tools for his spell.

And then was pretty sure he cast it wrong because, instead of detecting and showing him where Elspeth was, it brought the woman to him.

Chapter Twelve

Holding onto Babsy, perched on the sliver of a seat at the back of the bike—which Babette had apparently borrowed on the fly, AKA stole—Elspeth didn't have much time to think about Luc. Too much squealing in delight and yelling, "Faster!" as she hung on to Babette while they took tight corners and raced down straight stretches.

Elspeth did not have the time to process how Luc made her feel—emotionally. Her girly parts, however, felt very wet and tingly.

At least she wasn't alone in her attraction. His rather large erection had proven that. That kind of massive growth should be looked at. She'd volunteer.

For his health, of course.

When the bike slowed to a stop, she was ready to ask Babsy to turn around when she realized they'd not arrived at their hotel, but the airport.

"What are we doing here?" she asked.

"Time to go home."

"Home? I can't go home yet. I need to help Luc." Help him with his grief. Help him adjust to this world. Help him out of his pants.

"Luc can help himself."

"What of our luggage?"

"We'll buy new stuff," Babette replied. "We have to hurry. I have orders from your mother and the king to bring you home."

"How kind of them both to care. But—"

Babette interrupted Elspeth. "They miss you."

"They do?" Elspeth's expression brightened. "I miss them, too. But really, if Mother wants to see me, I could just video call her. The king, too."

"A call isn't like a hug in person."

"True." She could tell Babette was coming over to the hugging side. "But what of our mission?"

"You heard the Emerald cow, nothing to see."

Elspeth chewed her lower lip because she heard the lie. Did her bestie hide something from her? "You're still pining for Joanna, aren't you?"

"What? No." Babette acted startled, but Elspeth knew it was an act.

She patted her bestie's knee. "Don't worry. You'll find someone else. Someone who isn't married or a homicidal despot intent on ruling the world." Babsy's last girlfriend now lived in some alternate dimension with a huge tentacled monster.

Which, for some reason, made her think of Luc. Earlier, she'd collapsed in sadness because of his story. Now that she'd had time to recover, she found strength in it. Purpose. He might not realize it yet, but he needed her. Needed her to show him how to be happy again.

I have a mission. Which was why, when they boarded the plane, she excused herself right away to go to the washroom—and kept on going out the door before it closed.

She ran back into the airport and then out to the area with all the taxis, only to realize she'd misplaced her wallet. On the plane.

"Oh fiddlesticks." How would she get back to Luc?

She could always change shapes and fly, but this close to the airport, she'd probably get into trouble. The king had sent out a memo about them interfering with airplane flight routes.

She'd have to get farther away before she attempted it. Given walking was considered healthy, she set off with a jaunty step. A car pulled up alongside her. The window rolled down, and a very handsome man peered out at her.

"Can I give you a ride?" he asked.

The kindness of strangers never failed to delight. "That would be epic," she exclaimed. "How nice of you to offer."

She went to grab the door handle, only to pause as someone shrieked, "Elspeth Mary Canard, don't you dare get in that car!"

Oddly enough, that sounded just like her mama. A quick whirl showed Babette stalking down the sidewalk. She didn't seem to be enjoying the energizing walk, judging by her scowl.

Turning back to her Good Samaritan, she offered an apologetic smile. "Oops. I see my friend. I guess I won't need a ride, after all."

For a moment, she could have sworn the driver's

eyes turned red and, amidst the swirl of cologne, a hint of something else appeared. Something familiar…

He sped off just as Babette reached her, hands planted on her hips.

"What is wrong with you? We are supposed to be on a plane flying home."

"I told you, I have unfinished business here."

"Yes. Yes. You told me. Luc needs you. Blah. Blah." Babette rolled her eyes. A lot of people exercised their orbs in that way around Elspeth.

"This isn't just about Luc. It's also about the missing girls."

"What missing girls? The humans?"

Elspeth shook her head. "Nope. The dragon ones. Joanna lied to us."

"I knew it!" Followed by a crowed, "Told you so."

"And I should have believed you. Especially since it must have been hard to accuse her given your attraction."

Babette's lips flattened. The reminder of her impossible lust still hard to handle. "What made you change your mind?"

It was Elspeth's turn to exercise her eyeballs. "Because I had a vision, of course."

"A vision." Babette repeated this slowly. Probably to ensure that she remembered it forever.

"Yes. A vision." Elspeth began to walk back in the direction of the airport and the taxis idling by the curb. "I get them all the time, sometimes in my dreams."

"Dreams aren't real."

"Mine are. I know the future." Several versions, as a matter of fact. Which could get confusing, especially when she assumed certain things had come to pass. A certain election came to mind.

"You dream of the future?"

"Mostly. Sometimes the past."

"How come I'm just hearing this now?" Babette asked, her expression quite skeptical.

Having been on the receiving end of that quite often, Elspeth never took offense but rather celebrated the fact that her friend didn't take things at face value but questioned. Everyone should be so bright and inquisitive.

"Sorry I didn't tell you sooner. Mama says I shouldn't speak of it." From a young age, Mama had whispered, *"Never tell anyone about the dreams. They won't understand. Hoard those secrets."* It was why Mama said she needed the drugs.

"Your mother knows?"

"As well as the doctors. Although they think I'm cured. I stopped telling them when stuff was going to happen. I did feel bad though when Dr. Gump got puked on that day in the cafeteria." Elspeth, knowing it was coming, had sat in the far corner with her green Jell-O.

"If you're seeing things, shouldn't you be in some temple or something? Isn't that where the fortune tellers go?" Babette asked.

"Do you think I could be a gypsy fortune teller? Those hoop earrings are really awesome. Although I've never tried to dye my hair dark." Elspeth grabbed a curl and yanked it taut. "How would it look?"

"How about we forget the hair for a minute and go back to the dreams you have of missing dragons. What makes you think they're real?"

"Not real so much as possibilities. I see many paths the future can take." The branches were many and, oddly enough, converged with some acts only being small blips in the road. "Some futures have more divergences than others."

"What you're saying is the future is not set in stone. Cool," Babette replied.

"Why aren't you more surprised?" Elspeth asked. Then immediately answered her own question. "My mother told you I was special."

"Actually, Aunt Klarice told me to ignore anything weird you do."

"I am not weird."

"You have to admit, you have quirks."

Elspeth tossed her head. "I am unique. Did you know I can gnaw through braided rope in under three minutes?"

"A better question is, *why* would you do that, and why the fuck would you want to time it?"

"Why not?"

"More like, why me?" Babette grumbled. "Let's get back to the missing girls. The ones you're so worried about. Who are they?"

"Anyone and everyone."

"Are you trying to talk like a temple priestess? Plain English, please."

"What I mean to say is that the only real commonality between the missing people is their sex. All women. However, the ages vary." Elsie closed her eyes as she tried to remember the vague dream from the night before.

"You said they were dragons."

"And humans. The humans he tends to feed on right

away. The dragons he prefers to savor." Elsie swayed in place, the vision finally replaying, but this time, she controlled the pace of it. The talent of the Yellow. Not to fight or kill or burn, but to see the truth. History as it happened.

It drove some people mad.

Her mother was determined to ensure it didn't happen to Elspeth. Hence all the hospital visits. Mama hoped to find a chemical and psychological balance to help her hold on to her sanity.

It worked. Elspeth didn't need as many pills now to maintain her happy, as long as she abstained from alcohol. It undid all her training.

"Have you had any visions about me?"

Not one she cared to share. Elspeth intended to make sure that vision didn't come to pass.

What of your promise to Mama not to meddle?

That didn't count with friends. She wouldn't let Babette get hurt. And she needed Luc to ensure that happened.

At least with Elspeth having admitted her secret, Babette didn't argue much when Elspeth said they were going back to see him.

Her heart fluttered in her chest as the taxi approached his home. Wondering how he would react when he saw her.

Most people groaned and then pasted false smiles. Crazy Elspeth, who said the oddest things, who saw the good in the world. No one could handle it.

Until Luc. She would have never believed a man like him would even notice a girl like her. However, she'd seen it in a few visions of the future, their bodies entwined. Flesh to flesh. Joined as if one.

EVE LANGLAIS

She couldn't wait.

Entering his house, not bothering to knock—let Alfred have a break—she went to the library, knowing she'd find Luc there. Yet he didn't even lift his head to acknowledge her.

He seemed much more intent on his map.

Which was why she snuck up on him.

Chapter Thirteen

"Where is she?" Luc stared at the map. Quite uselessly, he might add, since nothing on it meant a damned thing to him.

But what else could he do when his location spell had failed?

Am I doing it wrong?

Luc had never performed a locating spell before. His access to materials in the cell had proven rather sparse. Therefore, his current knowledge on how to execute it was by memory alone, which could be, admittedly, faulty.

There existed a multitude of ways he might have bungled it, and he had nothing to use as a reference. He'd fled Hell too quickly. *I should have brought some of the spell books with me.* However, in his haste to avoid being trapped, he'd fled without supplies.

Staring at the mess on the table, he had to wonder where he'd failed. Didn't matter. He'd have to start over. Only one problem. He'd already used the last strand of hair he could find. A bright yellow one he'd found in his bed.

A place she'd surprised him.

The woman constantly stunned him, first by being the first dragon he didn't actively hate. On the contrary, he rather liked her. He also needed her. His cock nodded in agreement.

He frowned.

He needed her for practical reasons.

His cock again agreed.

Apparently, they'd have to chat. He'd make his cock spit out why he was being a traitor. But only after he'd found Elspeth.

"Where are you?" he muttered under his breath.

"Right here!"

The declaration from behind startled him. He didn't even think. Just whirled and held up his hand. Staving off an attack.

Something pulsed out from him, a wave of force. A power of some kind that sent Elspeth and Babette sliding back to the door, giving him some space.

Too late. Her scent lingered, and he barked, "How did you get in here?"

He really needed to invest in some guards. He wasn't used to people unexpectedly coming to see him.

But didn't you want to find her?

Yes. But he'd have preferred not to have possibly squeaked like a rodent when it happened.

Alfred peered around the edge of the office door and asked, "Is the master in need of my services?"

"Not anymore. My uninvited guests have already found their way inside."

"What—" Alfred stopped midsentence to utter his

own squeak of surprise as Elspeth's arms snaked around his staid servant.

The man's feet left the floor as Elspeth lifted him for a squeeze. "Alfred."

"Miss Elspeth. How delightful to see you again." The dry tone didn't sound very excited.

"Aw, shucks. Thanks." She swung Alfred around, hugging him tightly. "You are just too adorable when you pretend to be a butler."

"Because he is a butler," Babette remarked.

"No way. He's much too nice to be a stuffy butler, aren't you, Alfie?"

Elsie beamed at him, and Alfred, obviously terrified for his life, replied, "Miss Elspeth is too kind to an old man."

"You're too adorable. I think we should keep him, Babsy."

"Hoarding people is forbidden," Babette replied. "We had this discussion a few days ago, remember?"

Elspeth pouted. "I remember, all eleven times. And just so you know, there was one vision where you let me keep him."

"Not today, Elsie. Now put the nice man down."

"But I have more hugs to give." Elspeth pulled him closer, and Alfred's face achieved an interesting shade of mauve.

I should rescue him by offering to take his place. Get close to her. Hold her. Touch her. Strip…

Um, perhaps he shouldn't offer himself.

"Drop him. Now," Babette barked.

"Fine." Elspeth set Alfred down. He shot her an indignant look before exiting the room more quickly than usual.

"Why are you here?" Luc asked, casually flipping over the notes he'd made on the spell he'd been casting —and slightly modifying each time.

"Because blondie over here says we needed to talk to you." Babette jerked her thumb at Elspeth. "So, here we are." She leaned against a table covered in something Alfred called a kom-pewter. It had a screen like the television, yet Alfred could give it commands and have it obey by showing him knowledge.

According to his servant, all humans had access to this all-knowing entity known as Internet and its servant, Google.

It made Luc's task of ruling the world somewhat more daunting until he realized if he killed Internet, then he'd solve his biggest problem.

According to Alfred, Internet had tentacles around the world. He'd need an imp, or something along those lines that was electrical-based to fry it. But those weren't easy to find. The governments kept that magical science locked up.

He turned his gaze to Elspeth as she approached to lean over his map. "Whatcha lookin' for?"

Emasculate himself and admit the truth? Not today. He'd been learning some things from the television and Alfred, too. He needed to be tougher. Less transparent. Not easy, given his upbringing.

But the more he lied, the better he got. "Just plotting my first takeover."

"How many boroughs is that? Three, four? Piece of cake." Elspeth leaned lower, enough that the neckline to her top sagged. He caught a glimpse of swelling breasts.

He averted his gaze, cheeks flushed hot. "Why are you here?"

"Can't a girl want to come see her new friend?"

The word flummoxed him even as it warmed his blood further. "We are not friends."

"You're such a tease." Somehow, Elspeth managed to sidle around the table until she stood close enough to give him a punch in the arm.

"Why are you hitting me?"

"It's called a love tap, you pussy. Don't be so weird." Babette drew closer. "If you two are done flirting, I have some questions for the weird guy with the bowl of blood in his library. Whose blood is it anyway?"

Not knowing if his blood was valuable on this plane, especially to dragons, he lied. Twice in one day. Look at him getting humanized to fit in.

"It's from an avian creature we are eating for dinner. With mashed potatoes." Lovely fluffy things. Delicious with dollops of butter.

Elspeth clapped her hands. "Why, thank you."

Startled, he asked, "For what?"

"Inviting us to dinner. We would be delighted to accept."

"But when…" He paused, going over his words. "How…?"

Babette uttered a loud snort. "Don't argue, dude, just go with the flow."

"See, Babette. I told you we had to come here. Otherwise, we would have eaten another meal in a restaurant."

"But I like being served," Babette grumbled. "There're no dishes."

"Alfred will serve." The words cementing their invitation. He would have frowned, except Elspeth looked exceptionally pleased. "Was there a reason you were here, other than for nourishment?"

Elspeth shook her blonde curls. "Nope. I'm good. Just happy to hang with you."

"I can't believe you're going to make me do it," Babette grumbled.

"Do what?" Elspeth asked.

"You know what I have to do."

"No, I…" Elspeth's face turned dreamy for a moment, her eyes out of focus, her lips parted. A single crease marred her brow. "You didn't come here because I asked, and you didn't get off the plane for me." Elspeth's gaze narrowed in on Babette. "You came to ask him questions about the missing women."

"What missing women?" Luc asked.

"The ones she was ordered to ask you about." Elspeth shook her finger at Babette. "That's not nice. You let me think you came back for me."

"I would have anyhow. Probably."

Elsie raised a brow.

"I would have come back because your mother told me to watch your butt."

"Yet fear of Mama is not why you returned. You came to Luc's castle to grill him," Elspeth accused.

"Yes." Caught, Babette no longer denied it, and Luc listened carefully to glean as much as he could from the strange conversation.

"You lied to me. And I didn't even see it coming." Elspeth shook her head. Then laughed. "I knew you'd make a good bestie for a reason. It's not easy to fool me."

However, Luc had obviously fooled her. She thought

they were friends, and yet he would still plot the demise of her kind.

Eventually.

He'd have to master the demigod Internet first. And the microwave. Damned fire-breathing machine. They'd already had an encounter.

Luc hadn't won. In his defense, it was his first time. He'd thought it would be easy. He'd seen the machine used on the moving picture box. It seemed simple enough. He threw a lovely can with the red saucy noodles into its depths. Then he keyed in a sequence of beeping symbols and watched the light come on, and the carousel turn. The sparking inside proved exciting. The explosion after, rather unexpected. Worst part? The noodles were ruined, and it was the last can.

"Given you're now treating Luc as a suspect, I guess we can't use his castle as a base of operation." Elspeth tapped her lower lip.

A full lip. A suckable lip. He blinked and looked away.

"We're still staying here," Babette declared. "This place is nicer than a hotel. And if he's guilty of taking those women—"

"What women?" Luc snapped.

"—then we'll find our best clues here. DNA and scent and maybe even some panties, eh, Luc?" The accusatory side-eye drove his shoulders back.

"I haven't the slightest idea of what you speak." At all. Not surprisingly, Luc couldn't follow their logic.

"You say that, yet I know you're lying about this being chicken blood." Babette jabbed a finger at the ruined spell in the bowl. "I don't recognize the smell. What is it? And why is it in a bowl? Holy shit, dude, were you drinking it?" Babette's features pulled taut in repugnance.

Elspeth leapt to his defense. "Eating it from a bowl is much more sophisticated than the vampire method of chomping on some neck."

"At least a neck nibble is intimate and special." Babette waved a hand. "This is a little sloppy. I mean, where's his spoon? Crackers? And is that a hair on top?" She shuddered. "That's gross."

The mere thought of drinking it had him retorting. "I am not ingesting the blood. I was using it to scry for someone."

"Cry? Who died? Who were you crying for?" Elspeth reached over to him. Logic dictated he slip out of reach. Being near to her did something to him.

It seemed cowardly to avoid her, though; therefore, he allowed the hug. He just refused to enjoy it despite the warmth suffusing him.

She soothed. "Don't cry. I'm here. You are not alone."

Uncomfortable, he managed to mutter, "I was not crying. I was *scrying*. As in trying to divine the location of someone."

"Who are you looking for? Another victim?" Babette accused.

"As a matter of fact, I was looking for you. I have questions."

"Ask away," Elspeth said. "Anything you want. It's yours."

He almost said, "*I want you.*"

Babette saved the day.

Chapter Fourteen

"Dude and his questions are gonna have to wait," Babette declared. Despite being the shortest person in the room, Babette had no doubt about her importance.

"I, wait?" he managed an imperial lilt. "On the contrary, it is you who shall have to—ack."

A flying hellion jumped on him, taking him by surprise and throwing him against the table, hard. She held him by the shirt and shook, a small ball of fury. "Speak!"

"And if I don't?" he asked.

"Then you shall encounter my rage." Babette shook, her entire body bouncing, not budging him a bit.

He sighed. "Are you done yet?"

Jumping down, Babette tossed her head. "Not quite. We still need to talk about the missing girls."

"There is nothing to speak of. I am not responsible."

"Says you. Boss says we have to keep an eye on you. Watch your every move until we can clear you as a suspect."

"You plan to spy on me?" He seemed rather shocked.

"Spying is such a harsh word," Elspeth interjected.

"No, it's about right." Babette's lips curled into a smile, one that screamed: make war, not nice.

"You would blame me without proof."

"Why not? You've already stated you hate our kind." Babette tossed his words at him.

Arms crossed, Luc declared, "You are no better than your ancestors."

"Oh, I am *way* better than them, dude. Want to see?" Babette crooked her fingers.

Luc's expression darkened, and his forehead dimpled in two spots.

"Play nice, everyone." Elspeth placed herself between them, breaking the eye contact. Handling two besties was like wrangling playschool children. Get between them before the fists flew. She'd liked that job, getting to be with the younglings all day long.

Pity she hadn't kept the position long.

Letting a parent know she'd had a vision of their child riding a bike without a helmet and it not ending well saw her fired. Even worse? No one believed her, which led to Elspeth going off her meds for a few hours and slashing the tires on the boy's bike. Because of her intervention, the boy bypassed his horrible fate. He lived and she was pretty sure he wouldn't choose the future road where he turned into…no, best not think of that.

Babette pushed off a bookcase and stalked closer. "I don't see why I have to play nice. There are people missing. Dragons. Which means he needs to tell us now what he's done with the missing girls." Babette squinted at Luc.

He glared right back. "Again, I am going to ask, what missing girls? It is just Alfred and me in residence at the moment. I don't believe the cleaning crew is due until tomorrow."

"Are you saying they're dead?"

"Who's dead?" he barked. "You are speaking in riddles."

Elspeth could see his temper rising.

"He didn't do it." Elspeth rose to his defense. Her visions didn't tell whodunit, but they did give her a fair certainty that it wasn't him. Most of the time.

"Didn't do what?" he said with utter exasperation.

"Stop it with the innocent act." Babette shook a finger at him. "We know about the missing women. And given you kidnapped Elsie, you're the prime suspect."

He glanced at them, one after the other. "Are all your kind so mentally challenged? I have no idea of what you speak. Or whom. I've kidnapped no women."

"But you like locking them up," Babette accused, making Elspeth almost frown.

When she'd told her bestie about him pretending to abduct her, she'd emphasized the romantic aspects.

"Yes, I did initially imprison some of the staff upon my arrival. However, at Alfred's insistence, I released them."

"And buried their bodies so they wouldn't talk!" Babette accused.

"Again, you're talking in riddles, but if you're implying I am to blame, you're mistaken," Luc said.

"Where are these people you supposedly released?"

He shrugged. "I haven't the slightest inkling. Alfred helped me disperse them."

"Alive?"

"I would assume. I didn't oversee him personally, but you've met Alfred. Very capable for a human."

"Are you implying Alfred killed them?"

A snort emerged from Luc. "I highly doubt he could dispose of that many able-bodied specimens on his own."

"Alfred is tougher than he appears," Elspeth remarked.

"Since you can't vouch for the staff's continued health, who can?" Babette wasn't letting go.

"I can." Alfred entered the room, pushing a trolley with a steaming pot and cups, along with a plate of cookies. "Tea?"

"You saw these people leave alive, not as the walking dead or in body bags?" Babette asked, snaring a cookie before sitting and accepting a cup of tea.

"The master might lack some of the modern niceties. However, he is amenable to reason. When he realized there was no benefit in keeping them locked in the stalls, he told me to set them free. With severance."

"How kind." Elspeth beamed. However, Luc grimaced and rubbed his chest.

Heartburn? Poor thing.

Babette continued to scowl.

"Be careful about all that frowning. You wouldn't want the wrinkles to stay," Elspeth reminded her.

"I'm going to have skin like a baby's ass well into old age. You, on the other hand, probably won't live to know." Babette shook a fist.

"You're probably right," Elspeth agreed.

"Are you done with your questions?" Luc asked.

"Not quite." Babette eyed Alfred. "How do we know you're not lying for your boss?"

The butler stood straight with a hint of a smirk around his thin lips. "Would you like the names and addresses of the previous staff? I can easily acquire a list."

"That sounds great." Elspeth beamed. "See how well things can go when we work together."

"Don't get too excited yet. Just because he didn't kill anyone that could be traced back here doesn't mean he's not responsible for the others." Babette glared, and Alfred, with a harrumph, left the room.

"Are we still discussing this?" Luc flopped into a chair.

"Yes, we are, because humans are missing in this area. And according to Elsie over there, who apparently has voodoo dreams, dragons have upped and disappeared, too."

"Dreams?" Luc caught the word and glanced at Elspeth. "You mentioned that before. Do you have the true sight? The ability to see the future?"

"Only when I forget to take my pink pill."

"I never met any seers during my life, but I was taught about those who have visions of the future. It was a rare and dangerous gift that, for my people, resulted in death."

"Nice job not freaking her out, twat waffle." Babette rolled her eyes.

"You misunderstand. It is not the sight that killed them. In my world, the suzerain consumed anyone with the gift of foresight first."

"Hold on, shouldn't they have seen it coming?" asked Babette.

Elspeth shook her head. "We don't always see what we want. Our own death isn't always clear."

"Have you seen me?" he asked.

At his query, she almost blurted out her secret. *I've seen you for a long time now.* Just hadn't known it was him. Had seen them together in a few possibilities.

She'd also seen death.

Chapter Fifteen

The expression on her face said it all. *She's seen me in the future.*

Exciting, yet at the same time, suddenly, he wasn't so sure he wanted to know what the future held. What if… what if he failed?

Luc had travelled to this dimension for revenge, but the more he learned, the less likely it seemed. How could one demon take on a world of billions?

What if he aimed lower and stuck to his original plan of dragons only? If he asked Elspeth, would she know if he succeeded? Would she have a vision of him eradicating all the dragons? Of killing her friends and family? It occurred to him that he never wanted her to experience that, even in a vision.

"You don't have to tell me anything," he said. He preferred not to know. To go into the future making his own decisions and not trying to manipulate fate.

"It wouldn't matter if I did. There're so many possibilities. Even telling you creates a new path." Elspeth rolled a shoulder and pursed pink lips. The gloss on them a temptation he wanted to lick.

"Did you see my arrival in a dream?"

"Maybe." Spoken in a drawl.

He couldn't quite decipher the secret smile that lit her lips, but it warmed him.

Babette cooled his ardor. "She saw you coming, whoop-de-doo. I'm more interested in the fact that you arrived and people started going missing. Are you going to deny that you'd like all dragons to die because of a personal revenge plot?" Babette's gaze lasered him in place.

"No, I don't deny it. However, while I would like to take credit for the current missing dragons, alas, I have yet to truly embark on my vendetta. Probably because you are both the first dragons I've encountered since my arrival." And he just couldn't bring himself to kill them.

I'm weak. He knew his mother looked upon him with disappointment.

Yet, at the same time, he heard his father whisper, "*You are compassionate.*" He couldn't kill two innocents. The irony now was in them accusing him of murder.

"You're lying. You admit to being here to extermi-nate us. How many thus far?" When Babette would have stepped closer, Elspeth managed to body-check her.

"Talk with your lips, not your hands," Elspeth sang to her friend.

"I'd get better results if you'd let me chat with my fist," Babette grumbled.

Luc spread his hands wide as he shrugged. "Attacking me won't change the answer. I haven't killed anyone since my arrival." To his family's shame. "Not a single one. Contrary to your bloodthirsty belief, I do not go out of my way to murder things."

"What have you been doing then?"

"Mostly acclimatizing myself to your world and customs. There is much that is different in our culture that I've needed to learn in order to blend in."

"If you need help, I'll teach you!" Elsie waved her hand, her smile inviting, bringing to mind her closeness to him in bed.

I know what I'd prefer she teach me.

"Since you obviously don't have any real questions, now it's my turn," Luc said, turning away to focus on more important matters. "Explain to me more about your place in this world. According to Alfred, dragons have only recently announced their presence to the humans." Which, given the news reports he'd listened to, had some seriously violent tendencies. He'd be hard-pressed to declare who was more dangerous, humans or dragons.

"The revelation of our kind started with the shapeshifters, actually." Babette took on the role of teacher. "Some dude called Parker decided he was tired of living in secret and let the wolf out of the bag. Then, some other creatures kind of popped up to say 'hello.' The dragons meant to keep hiding. However, Voadicia began to act in the open and forced us out there, too. Now, everyone knows we exist, and it's causing issues."

Luc had no problem imagining that. "The humans want to kill you for centuries of subjugation?"

"Uh, no, they want to study us and create laws for us to co-exist," Babette said.

Elspeth disagreed. "They just want to be our friends."

"You are hopelessly naïve." Babette rolled her eyes. "The humans hate us. It's why we've hidden this long."

Luc's turn to frown. "You were hiding." This didn't jibe with his perception of dragons. Dragons took openly and without mercy. How bad were humans that the dragons feared them?

"We hid because it was the smart thing to do." Babette prowled the office, checking out the shelves.

"You hid out of fear." The very idea seemed astonishing to Luc. Dishonest, too.

Would he have to lie about whom he was to survive in this world? Would he, as the last surviving demon, be in danger?

"Sometimes, hiding is smart." Elspeth took on a softer tone. "It's a math thing, which, I'll admit, I'm not good at, but even I can get large general numbers. Lots and lots of humans. Few dragons. We don't want to do anything to spook them. The last time, with the help of dracinore—"

He interrupted. "The what?"

"Dracinore. Some kind of metal, not from this plane, that totally inhibits our ability to change."

His lips flattened. "I think I know of what you speak." He also knew what dimension it came from.

"With a stash of dracinore shaped into weapons, the humans almost managed to exterminate us."

"We got rid of that shit when the dragon mages were banished," Babette noted.

"Doesn't matter. If the humans feel we've become a threat, they won't need the dracinore. They've got the weapons now to annihilate us."

"Did a vision show you that?" Babette asked, head canted at an angle.

"I don't think that particular future will happen now that Remiel is in charge." Elspeth's eyes crossed. "As long as he's around, an unwary truce will exist between dragons and humans."

"Who is Remiel?" And why the sudden surge of anger at her evident admiration of the guy?

"He is our Golden king. The one foretold. Don't you know the histories at all?" Babette asked.

"I am not from around here."

"Luc is from the same place Voadicia emerged from," Elspeth confided.

"You came here from the hell world?" Babette's eyes widened.

"You know of it?"

"Yeah. My best friend Deka spent some time there with Samael. But they said that world was dead."

"It is. I was hidden away in a dungeon by the suzerain's minions. They needed one of the blood to access some of the spell books of my people."

"You're really from there?" Babette frowned as she walked around him, examining him. He kept his arms crossed and pretended insouciance. Let her look. She'd find nothing but perfection. His people might have lost many things, but their beauty was legendary.

Babette leaned in close for a sniff.

"He's like cinnamon," Elspeth confided. "At times, when his eyes get sparky, it's like cinnamon baked in an intense, dry sun. And other times, it's like he's a hot cross bun dribbled with icing." She licked her lips.

She's thought of my scent. Luc could barely contain his surprise at her description. He knew enough about cinnamon and icing that he understood she paid him a compliment.

Leaning in for a whiff, Babette didn't wax as eloquent. "Dude, you do smell funny. What are you?"

"Babsy! You can't just ask him that," Elspeth hissed. "It's rude."

"He's not human, and he's not dragon. Which makes him interesting, and I want to know." Babette perused him from head to toe. He preferred it when Elspeth did it.

He liked it even better when she stepped in front of him, the scent of her enveloping him. She smelled like pure sunshine.

"Don't put him on the spot. Maybe Luc can't tell you because he's some kind of rare thing. What if he's the last unicorn?

"A unicorn?" Babette snorted. "Those died out a long time ago. Eaten because they were tasty."

"As were dodo birds supposedly, but what if they simply went to another dimension?" Elspeth added.

"You think he's a dodo bird? I could see that." Babette arched a brow enough for him to grasp her reference to the avian creature was emasculating.

Elspeth's lips pursed. "Probably not from the bird family, given you don't have the right kind of feathery hair."

"Are you a selkie?

He had no idea what any of those creatures were. And he tired of hiding. About time someone of his kin showed pride. He thrust out his chest, shoulders back and declared, "I am a demon."

Babette eyed him up and down then shook her head. "No, you're not." Flat-out denial.

"I am."

"Then where are your horns and tail? What about your wings and gross, scaly skin?"

He blinked at her. "How do you know what we look like?" He had only seen illustrations. He'd yet to actually transform. He wasn't even sure he could, having lived amongst the poisoned metal in the rocks of the dungeon for so long.

He'd never been more shocked than when his mother managed to pop some horns and a few teeth.

"If you're going to lie, then you should have chosen something less distinctive. The Bible has been describing your kind forever."

His brow wrinkled. "What is a bible?"

"A religious text. I think the first one was done by the Christians. Or was it the Catholics?" Babette asked Elspeth, who shrugged replying, "I thought they were the same thing."

"The Christians?" He spat the word. "They are part of the group who banished us to that other realm." The demons found those sanctimonious fools tastiest of all. Part of the reason why the Christians banded with the elves to rid themselves of his kind.

"Why were you banished?"

At that, he smiled. "Because we were unapologetically violent."

"I'm surprised you went."

"The problem with being violent is that others are violent in return. We were never as populous as humans and, with our infighting, not anywhere near to being a cohesive unit. For a while, my ancestors rallied under the banner of the original Terrible One. I am named after him, the mighty Lucifer."

"Your boyfriend is named after the Devil," Babette stated to Elspeth flatly.

"I know. Cool, right?"

"Hell, yeah." Babette fist-bumped Elspeth.

"I thought you wanted my story." He frowned at their interruption.

Elspeth melted it with a smile. "Sorry. Please, tell us more. You're related to the Lord of Darkness, Lucifer."

"I am. He was felled in battle, which resulted in the demon legions being routed. The Christians gave my kind a choice. Leave or die."

"Kind of like what happened to the dragon mages," Elspeth noted. "Both sent to learn the errors of your ways. Looks like it worked."

"For the demons, yes. But not the mages. Our punishment changed us while in that other place." According to the history his father had taught him, they didn't have a choice. The demons started out in their hell world, reacting violently to everything and everyone, only to realize they would die out if they didn't change their ways. Which led to a revolution of their mindset. It helped that the very fabric of that other world stifled their magic and bestial side.

"By the time the dragons were exiled to Hell, my people had achieved a peaceful utopia. They no longer remembered how to fight. They no longer shifted into their demon self. They were a society based on trust and caring."

"Gag me." Skepticism thrived within Babette. "You expect me to believe you became some beatnik, drum-tapping, happy-go-lucky immigrants? I call bullshit."

"Babsy! Language."

"What?" Babette swung her gaze to Elspeth. "Don't

tell me you believe this crap. The guy speaks perfect English."

"The brothers who kept me hidden from the suzerain taught me." Television did the rest. Learning was something Luc did well.

"You expect us to believe you're the last of your kind?"

"If there are others, I knew not of them, nor can I return to search. The world has shifted. The portal is now closed."

"Convenient." Babette pursed her lips. "It means we can't even check out your story."

"Why would I lie about who I am and where I come from?" The idea baffled him.

"You tell me."

Elspeth interjected. "Let's just say he is a demon and the last of his kind. Shouldn't we be helping him adjust?"

"Have you lost what little pea-sized brain you had left? Maybe your mom is right, and you should stay on drugs." Babette rounded on Elspeth. "Have you not watched any movies about Hell or demons? Because I have, enough to know demons are bad dudes. It's in their nature to be violent."

If it was supposed to be in their nature, then he might be defective because, while Luc wanted to be violent and bloodthirsty, he'd yet to quite achieve that state. Being raised in a cell, and by a peace-loving father, he'd never had a chance to practice sparring. He'd only learned magic because of his mother's hidden lessons.

Thinking of his mother reminded him of his purpose. "Interesting that you admit a species can't change. Are you conceding then that you are like your ancestors?"

"You mean awesome?" Babette blew hotly on her fingers and then polished them on her shirt. "Yeah, we're awesome and smart and strong."

"Duplicitous. Selfish."

"Those, too."

"You admit then that a dragon's nature is to covet what others have and take it? By force if necessary."

"It's the rule of the strongest. Evolution, dude." Babette shrugged. "We can't help it if we're just genetically superior."

"Not all of us take," Elspeth interjected. "I don't."

Hadn't she, though? Since the moment they'd met, she'd taken his burning desire for revenge and replaced it with something far worse—hope for a future.

"You might not take, but that's because you're special. Hockey-helmet special," Babette muttered.

A remark he didn't understand. The conversation had veered wildly off track. "If your kind respects strength, then they will have no issue when I begin to draw armies to myself in preparation for my coup."

"His what?" Babette asked.

"Luc wants to rule the world." Elspeth clapped her hands. "Isn't it marvelous how someone who's had to overcome so much can still ascribe to wonderfully lofty goals?"

Babette shook her head. "More like suicide. You do realize he's just one guy."

"Demon," he corrected.

"Excuse me, demon. You're both delusional if you think a *demon* can rule the world. He'll be lucky if he's not captured and probed by government scientists." Babette snickered.

"I won't be captured." Not again.

"Because you're just that tough?" Babette mocked. "Your plan will fail, dude."

"Perhaps I won't kill the humans." There were too many, and he'd like to retire eventually. "But I won't be as lenient with dragons. For the sins of your ancestors, you shall die. All of you." Yet the moment he said it, he wanted to retract it, especially since Elspeth's face took on a sad cast.

"Dude, that's harsh. You almost made her cry."

He didn't need Babette's chiding to succumb to chagrin. "Perhaps some can be spared."

"He spared the rod, and the children revolted. They came after their gods and their kings." Elspeth spoke in an almost singsong voice, her eyes taking on a dreamy cast. "I see the armies gathering. The lives, the future of countries on a battlefield. Soaking it in blood. So much blood…" Elspeth snapped out of her vision.

Babette stared at her. "What the fuck was that about?"

Elspeth rolled a shoulder. "Sometimes, a certain future is stronger than others and becomes especially vocal when I'm around a focus person."

"A what?" Luc asked.

"It means shit happens around you, dude. Even I get that." Babette let her disdain shine through.

"There are many forks that depend on you," Elspeth noted. "It's sad how many end in death, though. Hasn't there been enough already?"

Yes. And if it were just him, he'd abandon his foolish

plan. Yet the moment he contemplated it, he could picture his mother's face and hear her last words.

He owed it to her. That didn't mean he said it aloud. His gaze caught on Elspeth's.

An outside force got between them. "Getting a little too intense there, dudes. Back up. Three feet. Or as the Catholic school told us, keep Jesus between you."

"You went to Catholic school?" Elspeth sounded surprised.

"Not for long. I got kicked out." Babette sounded quite proud.

He, on the other hand, thought it was awfully lucky that she'd gotten to live so freely. To choose an education and more.

All things I could do if I weren't busy getting revenge.

"Dude, I want to help you." Babette's offer seemed a little too smooth. "If you're so keen on killing all dragons, then why not start with her?" Babette pointed at Elspeth. "Go ahead. She's a dragon. And if she's been true to form, she's probably driven you nuts at this point. Kill her. Come on. I'll hold her down if you want. But I don't think we need to worry. She won't stop you."

"I won't," Elspeth said, her eyes big and shining. "If this is what you need to make peace with yourself, then I am willing to sacrifice my life."

The fool woman closed her eyes and tilted her head back, baring her neck.

How dare she make herself vulnerable to him!

"Don't do that," Luc growled.

"What's wrong, demon? I thought this was what you wanted," Babette taunted.

"Killing a defenseless woman"—one whose laughter and hugs warmed something in him that had been cold for so long—"isn't what I want, but what else am I to do? I made a promise."

"A promise to someone who is dead now. Who never imagined you leaving Hell." Elspeth placed her hand on his arm, and he tensed. "Had your mother lived and seen the possibilities of this world, do you really think she'd ask you to throw your life away for a vendetta that will result in your death?"

"You can't know that."

"All paths to vengeance lead to your end."

Chilling words from someone who claimed to see the future.

"What else am I to do if not exact revenge? My family is dead. My world is gone. I have no purpose. No meaning." Why bother? It wasn't as if anyone would notice his passing? He was tired of the loneliness. His shoulders drooped under the weight of his despair.

Then he staggered as Elspeth threw herself at him. "Don't you dare give up!" The full weight of her body slammed into him, and he had to grab hold of her to balance them both. "You do have something. You have me. I will be by your side for as long as I can. Find me no matter what. By sticking by my side, you will find closure."

"I thought we were supposed to keep him from killing himself, not giving him tips on how to hasten it."

Did Babette seriously imply that Elspeth's presence was somehow undesirable? She was the only person he could tolerate. Even Alfred grated on his nerves with his pompous airs. He thought quite highly of himself for a human who wore too much cologne.

Luc came to Elspeth's defense. "More people should emulate her."

"Thank you." She smiled at the praise and gave his arm a squeeze. She might as well have fisted his cock; that was where he felt it.

"It's the truth. You are the only dragon I've met that I admire."

Babette gagged. "I think I am going to be sick. Can we save the puppy-eyes lovefest for another time? I'm still dealing with the whole demon thing. Can we see it? Get naked and change."

"No." He practically barked the word.

"Why not?"

"Why don't *you* transform?" he snapped.

"If you insist." Babette did, a quick shift of skin to scales and massive size, filling the room, making a few of the more delicate items hit the ground with a crash.

Alfred would probably complain.

Her wings fluttered, sending even more things flying. "Stop that."

"You did ask her," Elspeth noted. "Isn't she gorgeous? I always envied the Silvers. My mom was a half one. My dad is a Vermilion. Me, I got canary yellow."

"I think the color yellow is beautiful." The words spilled from his lips with ease, and his cheeks heated.

She smiled and mouthed, "Thank you."

A trilling noise drew his attention to the dragon in the room. Kind of hard to miss.

Babette did make an impressive beast. Many handspans taller than he. Fatter, too. Yet, the research he'd managed over the years, questions Maedoc and his brother, Eogan, answered not realizing how Luc stored the information, let him know that, despite the girth, a dragon weighed no more than a human. Most of it was hollow weight. Not that Babette was just a balloon that could be punctured. Dragons still had organs and tissue and all the other things that made a living organism; it was just spaced more widely. The atoms not sticking as close, yet maintaining their structure and purpose.

The spaces between provided the buoyancy. The ability to become light enough that the massive wings folded at the back could keep them aloft.

Fascinating.

He reached out to touch, only to have Elspeth snare his hand.

"You might not want to pet her like a dog. Trust me. I almost lost a hand doing that," she advised.

"I've never seen one this close."

"Really? But you said the dragon mages held you prisoner."

"I also said the magic they used to extend their lives also perverted their nature. The energy they imbibed to extend their lives affected their abilities. Even their appearance."

"What do you mean appearance?" Elspeth asked. "Did she look deformed?"

A grimace pulled Babette's dragon features, and her next fluted words were sad.

"What did she say?" he asked.

"That Voadicia looked all too human, and she never suspected."

"That is because she would have absorbed things over time. Magical ability. Appearances. Even scent."

Elspeth wrinkled her nose. "You mean she can change into anyone she's eaten?"

"If they left a strong enough pattern, then, yes." But it took effort. And effort took energy. Luc's blob-like jailors obviously conserved theirs to survive rather than look presentable.

"Can you change into a bunch of different shapes?" Elspeth asked, holding his hand in hers.

"No. Not even my demon self." The truth escaped. No time to take it back.

"But your horns…"

"An aberration. My people forgot how to become. Our world was comprised of a metal that impeded that ability."

"The dracinore," Elspeth said excitedly. "It's the dragon kryptonite, as well."

"Obviously not as severe, though. The suzerain had no issues using magic."

"But you said it yourself, her magic was perverted. Augmented by outside life forces. Who's to say that's not why she could circumvent it?" Elspeth said.

Luc frowned. "I guess it's possible."

The silver dragon fluted a high note then a low one.

Elspeth frowned. "No, that does not mean we should gather the remaining dracinore in this world and get it ready. It's not Luc we have to worry about."

"It's not?" He couldn't help his surprise.

A suddenly naked Babette appeared, and he averted his gaze.

"What do you mean it's not him we have to worry about?"

"Because he's not our biggest threat."

"Then who is?" Babette asked. "And you can look again, dude. I covered the girly bits. You don't have to be scared."

Heat injected his skin. "It's called respect." When younger prisoners filled the cells, privacy was almost nonexistent. But they did their best. A nude body became the equivalent of the words, "*I need to be alone.*" Everyone averted their gazes while it lasted.

Those who didn't? The hotheads and those that thought it acceptable to disrespect? Volunteered the next time the suzerain came looking for food.

Allowing his gaze to return, he noted Babette wrapped in a blanket, her shoulders bare but respectable by the measures of the time and place he found himself in.

Nothing was as expected.

"You still haven't said who's more dangerous than your demon boyfriend," Babette stated.

Boyfriend? He knew enough of the term to realize it implied a romantic attachment to Elspeth. Not exactly a repellent idea.

"I can't see the face of our enemy." Elspeth shrugged. "He's a magic user, that's all I know."

"A dragon mage," Luc said with a sneer.

"Or a demon," Babette retorted.

"Doesn't matter either way. Whoever that person is, they're the true menace and the reason Luc has to stick close to me."

"You don't need him to kill anything." Babette jerked a thumb at Luc. "You're a big girl. You can do it yourself."

"Not according to my visions. I need help. His help." She cast him an apologetic look. "Without fail, if Luc doesn't come to my rescue, I will die."

Chapter Sixteen

Tell people you'd seen yourself die, and there was always a ton of drama.

The first time it'd happened, Elspeth was six and having a party. Mother had planned it and invited Elspeth's whole kindergarten class, trying to make her strange daughter some friends. Elspeth went along with it because, in one vision, the party ended well.

However, someone must have crushed a butterfly somewhere because she didn't live in that version of the future. That morning, Elspeth had drawn a series of pictures. The yard, bright and green with growth. The pretty, white gazebo with its calming, limestone flooring. The brilliantly colored bouncy castle Mother had bought. And lots of happy, smiling faces. Elspeth was in the castle, waving while eating cotton candy.

The next picture showed a tornado suddenly arriving in the yard. Mouths on the people open wide in silent screams.

The next, a raging force, the entire page covered in vicious swirls of back and gray wax. Shredded within it, brighter colors. Then, the more disturbing parts…as in limbs. She'd worn her red crayon down to a nub.

Mother took one look at her art and calmly cancelled the party.

Elspeth had pouted. At six, she didn't grasp death. After seeing the destruction the tornado left in their yard, she'd gotten a slight inkling.

The party wasn't the only time she'd escaped death. Every few years, a new deadly vision would come along. Most could be avoided, and for those that couldn't, she asked for help.

Like now. She needed Luc to survive what was to come.

She'd not seen it clearly yet, just bits and pieces. What she'd not expected was her bestie's jealousy that Luc was pivotal to Elspeth's future instead of Babette.

"What do you mean you need this asshat to live? You know, I've been nice, trying to give you the benefit of the doubt with this whole vision thing. But now, I think maybe you're just deranged. Because who in their right mind would choose a demon over me to save them?" Babette shook her head and *tsked*.

Luc came to her defense. "Elspeth is not deranged. She has a gift. A rare talent."

"I don't know if I'd use the word gift," Elspeth muttered. Without her pills, remaining positive proved a touch harder than usual.

"It is a gift. Ignore the skeptics." A pointed look at Babette by Luc. "And don't doubt your sight. After my people changed their violent ways, they ditched many of our old teachings, too. They chose to ignore our seers when they should have listened."

"People have a hard time listening," Elspeth replied.

And using a bullhorn to get her point across was considered a public nuisance by the cops.

"Can you blame them for shutting their ears? You're talking about the future coming to you in dreams. I've dreamed, too, after eating some magic 'shrooms. Dreamed I was gonna date a despot who wanted to rule the world." Babette's face twisted. "Shit, that did happen."

"I don't need anyone to believe what I see. Because it's not always set in stone. There are many possible futures, and I don't see them all. Not even a fraction. Just chunks here and there. Sometimes, only a blink of an eye. Hints, certainly not enough to run around screaming that the sky is falling."

"Is it ever going to fall?" Babette asked with utmost seriousness.

"Not in anything I saw recently. But I believe there was a time back in the nineties where it almost happened." Mama claimed it was the big hair and the aerosol sprays in the eighties that almost caused it.

"Does anyone know you have visions?" Luc asked. In the dungeons, those with the gift tried to hide it. Because the suzerain always took those people away.

"My mother knows. Why do you think I spent so much time at the asylum growing up? Lovely place. Always a ton of art supplies." She fondly remembered their pudding.

"Erm, I thought the whole locked-away thing with some head shrinks had to do with your happy, happy attitude and lack of arrogance." Babette held out her hand and took the garments Alfred silently dropped into her palm.

An excellent manservant who arrived just in time

and, obviously, well prepared, given he'd managed to find women's garments rather easily.

Luc turned his head before Babette dropped the blanket.

Adorable.

"Dealing with my lack of arrogance and other dragon traits was only part of it. The dreams were the other reason. I started having the visions when I was young. Small things at first. Lost trinkets that I would see in a dream and then find. Knowing when someone was cheating on his or her spouse. Or lying. I thought I was doing the right thing by helping people and telling them." Elspeth's lips turned down. "People don't want the truth."

"They hurt you." Luc practically growled the word.

Startled, she raised her gaze to his and found herself captured by the blazing heat. "They didn't mean to."

"Why did your parents not protect you?" He paced, his body tense.

Also wearing entirely too much clothing. Really, who needed a shirt inside? Perhaps if she stripped hers, he'd remove his.

"My mother protected me. Once she knew what was happening, she told me that I had to keep those dreams to myself." At night when her mama smoothed back her hair, she'd whisper, "*Hide what you are. Tell no one. Trust me. It's best.*"

"How is that helping?" Luc stopped and whirled to growl at her.

"Because if people knew, they'd try to use me." The history she'd dug up on her kind was very clear on that point. "There's a reason Yellow dragons are rare." Rare and not long-lived.

Did something in her tone change? Because his gaze narrowed. "You're hiding something."

"Me?" She batted her lashes. He didn't soften. "You caught me. I have a twenty in my bra." She shoved her hand into her shirt and removed a green piece of paper. "I borrowed it from Babette in case we got separated again."

He swallowed. His eyes lost focus. Was he having a vision, too?

Babette snapped her fingers. "Dude, the way you're acting, people will think it's the first time you crushed on a girl."

What if it was? Elspeth had heard enough to know he didn't have much contact with people before coming here.

Luc rubbed his chin, mulling over everything they'd discussed, looking rather handsome and thoughtful. She could see the moment clarity hit him because his eyes widened and he blurted, "The person in your visions, the one you deemed more dangerous than me, is going to come after you."

"It's what seems most likely from what I saw."

"But that means you're in danger. Why haven't you departed? The peril is great if you remain."

"It's dangerous for me everywhere. The visions don't leave because I move around. The future doesn't stop if I'm not there."

"It's a large burden," he said softly.

"I guess, but I'm used to it." Elspeth smiled. "Good thing I'm a big girl. I can handle it."

"You shouldn't have to." Luc's growled words wrapped her in a caress. "No one should have to see the ugliness of the world all the time."

"It's why I have the pink pills. The green ones are for when my pink pills aren't working."

"You're on drugs?"

"Several," Elspeth admitted. "Or I was. I kind of stopped taking them a few days ago."

"Is that bad?" Babette asked. "Do you need a hospital?"

Elspeth cocked her head. "I'm not technically ill. I'll just be seeing more stuff until I get my meds back."

"Seeing…as in?" Babette queried.

"The future. We're coming to a right fork soon. Racing and racing onward and further." Elspeth cocked her head. "In some futures, we're heroes."

"Heroes?" Babette straightened. "With cool costumes?"

"The coolest."

"And you saw this?"

"Yup."

Babette cocked her head. "Question? Are all Yellow dragons psychic like you? Because this is the first I've heard of it."

"Because it's usually a weak power. Most Yellows barely get déjà vu, a few, like me, are inundated with possibilities and go quite insane."

"Are you crazy?" Babette asked. "Not that I'm judging. I like crazy."

She showed them a wide smile. "I'm a manageable crazy. I learned at the asylum that I could handle anything if I tackled it with a positive attitude and a grin."

"Are you sure they didn't mean positive attitude and a gun?" A dry reply by her bestie.

"Babette! Shooting is never the answer."

"I don't know if I agree with that. I've shot many a pheasant that was the answer to my aching belly."

"Your kind still hunts to eat?" Luc asked.

"Actually, we usually hit the grocery store unless I'm craving something really fresh."

"Did your people hunt?" Elspeth found herself curious about him.

"As my people evolved from a violent species to a peaceful one, we moved away from eating flesh. We chose to only eat that which we could grow and stopped hunting entirely."

At that Elspeth interrupted. "So you're saying you don't eat meat then?" Her nose wrinkled. "That doesn't seem right because I know I've smelled bacon in your house." She could scent the ambrosia of the salty protein from several blocks away.

"I eat meat. All my people ended up returning to it. In the dungeon, we didn't have a choice. When the jailors slowed our feeding, we hunted anything that moved."

"Meat is meat," Elspeth noted. "You survived."

"Hold on a second." Babette jumped in. "I want to know how you plan to fight. If your people didn't kill anything, then what method did you plan to employ to take over the world? Were you going to have a dance-off?" Babette did a finger snap thing, her body undulating as she sassed Luc.

He frowned. "Demons don't dance."

"And they don't fight either, according to you," Babette poked.

"Are you implying we were somehow less than you? I'll have you know, we were extremely advanced as a society."

Babette immediately fired back. "Did you have the internet?"

"No."

"Television? Cell phones? Dishwashers?"

"No. We had scrying mirrors, echo chambers, and washed our own dishes."

"But you didn't have any science," Babette exclaimed in her aha moment.

"Because we had magic."

"Except you didn't have magic. You said the metal in the rock made it impossible."

"I said it made it hard. In the dungeons where it was concentrated, it was nigh impossible. But aboveground, with some insulation from the effect, small things were doable."

"What about here?" Babette, ever sharp, quickly zoned in on the important bits.

He rolled his shoulders. "There is magic here for the shaping, but I don't yet know if it is compatible with me."

Luc's honesty was almost too much. Did he not know how to keep a secret? Elspeth wanted to tell him to keep some things to himself.

"As a representative for the demons, you are really starting to disappoint," Babette declared with a sigh. "You can't shift. You can't do magic. You can't have sex like a normal man."

"My ability to fornicate is fine," he exclaimed hotly.

Babette smirked. "Thank you." And then turned to Elspeth. "You're welcome."

"For what? I already knew we were compatible." She'd had a vision of them together.

"You get dirty dreams, too?" Babette's gaze widened.

"Not about other people," Elspeth quickly corrected, only to realize that it sounded just as bad. Her cheeks heated, and she couldn't look at Luc.

"You go, Elsie!" Babette high-fived her. "And I guess now that I know you're a true-blue gypsy lady with visions, I will forgive you for being freakishly happy and optimistic all the time." Babette's eyes lit up. "Fuck me, that's why you're so bloody nice. You're compensating for being fucked-up."

Elspeth's lips quirked. "That's only part of it. By doing unto others, I am trying to do my part to ease the ugliness in the world." She hung on to a vision of the perfect world, glimpsed only once. But it had stuck with her. "Most of the things I see, the bad stuff, is easy to avoid. Uttering a kind word instead of an insult. Sharing instead of hoarding."

"I am not sharing my hoard."

Elspeth put a hand on Babette's tense arm. "There is nothing wrong with having treasures. Simply ensure they harm no one."

"The only thing hurting is my ass from the candy."

"What do you hoard?" Luc asked.

Usually, she didn't tell. Elsie knew all too well the mockery people felt compelled to dish out. But she wasn't ashamed of her hoard, and Luc wasn't like a dragon. "I like to gather kind acts. Laughter. I find my collection of hugs especially satisfying."

Babette wrinkled her nose. "Those are emotions, not things."

"They are. And to me, they are the most precious things in the world." When she felt especially morose and disconnected, or if a vision hit her particularly hard, she'd retreat into her vault of hugs and fall back into the sensation of holding someone against her. Someone anchoring her to a place and time.

Not everyone understood that kind of treasure.

The look on Babette's face proved amusing. Bafflement. "You collect feelings. How are you supposed to touch and pet them? And eat them even if you're on a diet?"

"I remember them, and I feel good." Elspeth closed her eyes.

"What happens when you don't feel good?" Luc asked.

Her eyes opened. "We don't talk about that in my family."

Babette cackled. "Elsie, that was just about the funniest thing you've said all day. As if you're dangerous. Only around a dessert bar."

"You don't think I can kick ass?" Elspeth tittered.

"I know you can."

"We'll soon find out."

"What?" Luc yelled.

"You got an outfit planned?"

"Yes. It's hanging in the closet at the hotel. Or, at least I assume it still is."

Babette sighed. "Yes, that monstrosity is still there. I'd hoped to be thousands of miles away from it at this point."

The woman carried on a conversation as if Elspeth weren't discussing her eminent demise. She'd gotten used to people placating her and pretending she was joking.

Luc took it quite seriously. He glared. "Am I the only

one who grasped what Elspeth said? She predicted her death."

"And even she said she's wrong sometimes. Besides, she's a dragon. We're tough to kill," Babette remarked.

"Show a little care. She's your friend," he growled.

"Yours, too," Elspeth added. Then again, the mere fact that he felt the need to defend her said volumes.

"Chill, dude." Babette blew a raspberry. "You do realize now that we know about her future, we're going to stop it."

"How? We don't even know what we're fighting. How do you battle the unknown? Really, I'd like to know because it might help with the whole conquering thing."

Babette puffed out her chest. "Doesn't matter what it is. We'll go in and kill it."

"And that will solve all your problems?" he asked.

"It might have solved yours if you'd tried it," Babette retorted.

"Maybe it would have. Or, we would have all died that much sooner."

Elspeth didn't like his pessimism. It was up to her to raise his spirits. Or at least show solidarity. "Don't listen to Babsy. She's an instigator. I, on the other hand, am a peacemaker. I will turn the other cheek before I fight."

"What if they slap the other cheek?"

"I offer to forgive them because they are obviously hurting and in need of an outlet." And slaps didn't sting for long. It also made her cheeks naturally pink. It didn't take much to convince someone to slap her. They were always so helpful when she asked.

Luc scowled at her. "Speaking from experience, I can tell you that is a horrible philosophy. Sure, it sounds great on the surface, but here's the thing. If a person is willing to slap someone who's defenseless over and over, then there is no amount of forgiveness that will help. One day, you'll end up dead. My people learned that lesson."

"For me, managing forgiveness and creating my own happiness stave off the depressing nature of the visions. Without optimism, I tend to react poorly."

"You mean like when you're drunk? You're a right psycho when you've had a few too many," Babette remarked.

Heat rose in Elsie's cheeks. "Which is why I avoid alcohol. Apparently, when my inhibitions are lowered, some of my baser instincts emerge."

"You mean your dragon side," Babette interjected. "You're repressing your true self with all that goody-two-shoes shit."

"I don't need to be mean to be a dragon."

Hands planted on her hips, Babette sassed, "Maybe if you were mean, people wouldn't pick on you all the time."

"You don't pick on me."

"Don't look at me as a shining example." Babette ducked her head. "I'm one of those who made fun of you behind your back."

"I know, and I forgive you, best friend."

"Ack!" Babette gagged then sighed as Elsie insisted on giving her a hug. "I'll never understand you."

"That's okay. Because I've seen into your heart. You're a good person, Babette Silvergrace, and soon, you're going to find that special someone you've been looking for."

"You had a vision."

"No, I just know you will because you're so awesome."

Babette rolled her eyes, but she didn't sound angry when she said, "I think I'm getting a cavity from all this sweetness."

"I'm feeling nauseous myself," Luc announced. "If you feel the need to get emotional, kindly do it off the premises."

"Don't get your demonic thong in a twist," Babette drawled. "I'm leaving, but not because you want me to, dude. I gotta go report to the big boss."

"The king?" Elspeth asked to clarify.

"Duh."

"Are you going to announce my presence?" Luc's gaze turned dark and impenetrable.

"Yes. I can't keep a supposed demon a secret, but contrary to what you think, we're not out to get you. That was Voadicia's gig, not ours. Not to mention, now that I've met you, I can vouch for the fact you're not ready to take over the local gym, let alone the world. Ready, Elsie?" Babette looked at her expectantly.

"I'm not leaving yet."

"But your meds—"

"Can wait. I need to stay here."

Babette sighed. "Your mother won't like it."

"Mama will have to understand I'm old enough to make my own decisions. No more arguing. I'm staying, and you're going. We both know you can't make me leave. And you didn't have a problem with Luc and me being together before. While I was unconscious."

"That was before he was suspected of being a kidnapper."

"I haven't kidnapped anyone," he reiterated.

"Says you."

"Says me." Elspeth lifted her chin. "I am perfectly safe with Luc."

Babette's face contorted. "According to you. If I leave you alone with him and he turns out to be a murderer, your mother will crucify me."

Elspeth grabbed her bestie by the arm and began marching Babette to the door. She ducked close enough to whisper, "If you don't leave, I'll fulfill the vision where I kill you for being a cock-blocker."

"What? You're getting rid of me to have sex with him?" The woman tried to dig in her heels, but Elspeth just picked her up and kept walking.

"What of it? He's hot. Eligible." *I think.* She'd never seen a ring or a missus. "He's not scared of me. Did I mention hot?"

"Are you really going to allow yourself to think with your va-jay-jay at a time like this?"

"Yes. When else will I get this chance? Do you think I meet guys like Luc every day? Not all of us are petite and gorgeous like you."

Babette tossed her head. "Good point. It is easy for me to get laid."

"Exactly. Which is why you're going back to report. Without mentioning my being here with Luc."

"Use protection."

"Yes, Mother."

Babette grimaced as she paused before the front door. "This is probably a bad idea."

"Think of it as a good idea. The very best."

"If this goes to shit, I'm blaming you."

"It won't go to shit." *I hope.* Once Babette had left,

Elspeth shut the door, locked it, and leaned against the wood.

It was just she and Luc now. At last. She didn't quite run back to his office, but her walk occurred at a rapid pace.

She entered to find him staring out the window, his body rigid. She could practically see the tension oozing off him.

"You're angry," she stated.

"I'm always angry."

"Yes, but right now, you're angrier than usual." He trembled. A big, sexy man, so full of rage and hurt. She could see it. Feel it. She wanted to soothe it away. To kiss it better. Yet, she held back.

Touching him also had the effect of making her forget herself. Losing control…not always a good idea.

He whirled from the window, his eyes blazing blue, the skin on his forehead dimpling. "Why do you care how I feel? And don't feed me a line about caring about me. You don't know me."

"I want to."

Someone, though, wanted to wallow. He turned back to the window. "Go away."

"After the trouble you went through trying to find me?"

"Who says I was looking?"

"You did. Not to mention, that does." She pointed at the map and then the bowl of blood with its lone strand of hair. Her hair she'd wager. "You were looking for me."

"I was looking for a dragon to kill."

"Really?" She cocked her head, unafraid. He lied. But why? "I know you don't want to kill me."

"On the contrary, I do. Intently."

"Okay." She tilted her head back and bared her neck. "Let's do this again. Kill me."

"Stop toying with me."

"I'm not the one saying one thing and doing another."

"Killing is messy, and I like this shirt."

"It's plaid."

"And?"

"It won't show the blood after you wash it." She knew from experience.

"Would you stop trying to convince me to kill you? I don't want to." He crossed his arms and jutted his lower lip mulishly.

She wanted to grab hold of it with her teeth and suck for a while.

"You don't want to throttle me because you like me."

"Not in the least. I'll kill you when I'm ready. Which isn't now. You might as well leave. It won't be tonight."

She took a step closer. "Leave a friend in need? You should know by now, I can't do that."

"We are not friends."

"Of course, we are, silly. Especially now that we've shared our secrets and I've seen your horns. They're peeking again."

His hand partially rose then fell. "It is because of this you should leave before I come to my senses and kill you."

"Kill me? That seems a little extreme, don't you think? Yes, I know you say you want to rule the world, and I did see your impressive pecs—"

"Pecs?"

"—but it's not as if I took a picture of your hot body

and disseminated it over the internet as a meme titled *Demon Hottie*."

"Why would you want an image of my body?"

"To show off, of course. You are sexy."

"I am?"

"And hung." He couldn't hide his interest, not in those pants.

Luc's gaze narrowed. "By hung, you mean?"

She glanced down, and he followed her gaze to his covered groin with a crease between his brows.

"Am I not a standard size?"

"Don't you know? Surely, you and the other boys had penis competitions?"

He grimaced. "I don't have much experience with people."

Poor thing. While she didn't understand being socially awkward, she could empathize with not having a large circle of friends.

"You have me now." She hugged him. Tried to give him a super-duper hug, the kind that would lift him off the ground and make him feel special, except he was too heavy. She settled for squeezing him—and groping his fine ass.

He was completely choked with emotion when he said, "What are you doing?"

"Hugging the sadness out of you."

"I am not sad."

"Depressed."

"Not depressed either. But if you are looking for a term to describe me, homicidal comes to mind."

"Oooh, who do we need to kill?"

"We?"

"Of course, *we*. I told you, we are friends, and

friends don't let friends murder alone. You tell me when and where, and I'll bring the shovel."

"You do realize I haven't given up on my plan to kill all of dragonkind for eradicating my race?"

"I know, and I'd say you have a good reason. I'd hate me, too."

He sighed. "I don't hate you. However, I promised my mother I'd seek revenge."

"You know, if you want that to sound really cool, you should say it more like this." She struck a proper pose and recited from her favorite movie. "Hello. My name is Inigo Montoya. You killed my father. Prepare to die."

"But you didn't kill my father. And I thought your name was Elspeth."

"It is. I'm just saying…you know what, forget explaining. We need to watch it."

She grabbed him by the hand and dragged him downstairs to where she'd seen a television when exploring.

They were halfway through the movie *The Princess Bride*—which she'd found on some streaming channel—with her snuggling against him, her hand on this thigh, when he turned to ask, "Do you have a mate?"

Given it came out of the blue, it could only mean one thing. "Can't stop thinking about me either? I know the feeling." He consumed her thoughts.

"Is it a spell?"

She shook her head.

"Then what?"

"Attraction. You're the PB for my jelly."

He frowned.

"Peanut butter?"

He still looked confused.

"I'll show you what a PB&J is later. Right now, I think this is better suited."

She leaned forward and kissed him.

Elspeth kissed him—and kissed him alone because he froze.

Solid.

She wasn't even sure he breathed.

A tug at his lower lip wrought a shudder in him. A lick of the seam definitely made him shiver.

"Are you going to kiss me back?" she asked, fingers wrapped in his hair.

"We shouldn't."

"Tell me to walk away, then." She snuggled closer, her ass in his lap, the hard pressure of his erection proof that he didn't want to stop.

"You are my temptation. My undoing."

Sexiest thing a man had ever said. Cupping his cheeks, she kissed him again, pouring some of her passion into it. Not too much. She didn't want to frighten him. *Watch your strength.*

Turning in his lap, she straddled him, her thighs on either side of his, more fully pressing his erection against her.

She rocked against it, and he stiffened again, only for a moment before his hands gripped her around the waist. His lips parted finally with a hot exclamation.

If before she was in control, that now changed. As if he'd unleashed it, his passion rolled out in a hot and sultry wave. She felt the fever of his skin. The possessive dig of his fingers into her flesh. The wet play of his tongue against hers.

She continued to rock against him. Building that pressure and—

"Ahem." Alfred cleared his throat as he walked in. He stood staring at a spot on the wall while Elspeth gaped at him, her lips—both sets—full and aching. "Would the master and his guest like some refreshments?"

Given someone elected to chaperone, she did her best to smile and act normal. "Hey, Alfie. Some drinks would be great."

"Privacy would have been better." Luc displayed an amazing ability to spin his head almost 180 degrees.

"If the master wishes privacy, then perhaps he should partake of private matters behind closed doors."

The starch riposte had Luc grumbling, "Perhaps smart-mouthed humans should keep their opinions to themselves lest I decide to eat them." He scowled and crossed his arms.

Adorable really, especially as she grasped that he was miffed Alfred had interrupted what promised to be an excitingly intimate moment between them.

"Got any popcorn, Alfred?"

"Indeed, I do. I'll fetch some."

"What is popcorn?" Luc asked.

"You'll see."

The moment was awkward. Elsie wanted to reach out to Luc, but he'd slid out from under her and moved to the opposite end of the couch.

He still sat there when Alfred returned with their snack.

When Luc eyed the popcorn with suspicion, Elspeth threw a handful at him. "It's good. Try it."

"You try it." He tossed a puffed piece back, and

Elspeth dove to catch it. She hit the floor, tucked and rolled, popped up and opened her mouth, tongue extended.

"You caught it!" Luc exclaimed. "My turn."

Which was how Babette found Elspeth dodging around the room, mouth open, laughing as she tried to catch popcorn and giggling when it bounced off her nose.

Even more astonishing, how handsome Luc was when he finally cracked a smile. Panty-wetting, knee-weakening gorgeous.

Now that Elspeth had cracked the smiling barrier, next, she needed him to kiss her. Kiss her with all the passion she knew he kept bottled inside. She hoped it happened soon so she could die happy.

Because the end was creeping closer. She'd seen it in a vision. A single revelation. Given she was off the drugs, it usually meant the options were narrowing. Soon, there would be only one outcome.

Now if only she could see ahead to find out if she survived.

Chapter Seventeen

The interruption by Babette proved annoying and fortuitous.

Luc couldn't recall a more carefree moment. A happy moment. And it was because of Elspeth. A dragon.

More than ever, he found himself torn. The need for revenge warred with his enjoyment of being in her presence. His urge to touch her. His desire to kiss her…and more.

He couldn't forget the embrace they'd shared. A kiss that had left him tingling and craving.

Yet, once again, before he could forget his past, someone just had to interrupt.

"Elsie, stop playing with the demon and come with me."

"What for?" she asked, throwing a piece of popcorn overhead and then sinuously moving her body to catch it.

"Our king needs us for something."

"A mission?" Elspeth's gaze brightened, and she

straightened. "Sweet. We'll be ready to leave—"

Babette shook her head. "He can't come. Dragon business."

The stark reminder had him stiffening. "As if I want to be involved. Go. I have other things to do." Like planning the demise of the world. Perhaps placing an advertisement for some soldiers. *Wanted: Mercenaries for my legion to take over the world.*

Arms crossed, he put on his most forbidding mien, which Elspeth ignored as she approached him and placed a hand on his tense forearm. "Sorry, I guess I have to go. I'll be back later, though."

He detected no lie in her words, and yet a chill settled over him. "You needn't bother. I'll be otherwise occupied."

"Don't have too much fun without me," she whispered before brushing a light kiss on his mouth.

Then she was gone, leaving him frozen once again. The allure of her scent and touch acting as a paralyzing spell.

He shook his head as Alfred entered.

"I see the ladies departed."

"Dragon business."

"Sounds serious. Especially given their earlier accusation that you might be involved in the abduction of women."

"You think their business is related to that?"

"It seems likely."

Also dangerous. Someone was abducting females. Elspeth was female.

He scowled. "They didn't want me to join them."

"The dragons are a secretive lot," Alfred stated. "I've been reading up on them since our meeting; however, I haven't found much. They keep their secrets closely guarded."

If only Luc had the wings of his ancestors. He could have followed. Thus far, he'd only managed a faint impression of horns.

But he did have magic.

Elspeth had interrupted his earlier attempt to scry for her presence, which meant he had all the tools he needed to find her.

He also had something better than a dead strand of hair. He snared the bowl with popcorn seeds, a few of them wet with saliva when she'd spat them out.

Rushing them to his library, he tipped the seeds into a clean bowl. The knife he'd taken from the kitchen sliced his skin easily, and his blood emerged, a dark blue liquid at first, turning to a deep burgundy the longer it was exposed to the air.

The bowl filled, the liquid covering the seeds. While it was still warm, he cupped the container and lifted it.

He closed his eyes. Pictured Elspeth. With her golden curls and bright smile. Remembered her sweet scent. Then whispered the words of magic. He knew them. He'd memorized them when still young. What else was there to do in the cells but learn and listen? The older ones did their best to pass on the knowledge so it wouldn't die if they did. He really should take the time to write the history of his people.

He realized he held the bowl of blood aloft. Distracted after doing the spell, he thought he'd failed again. Perhaps he'd missed a vowel. Or his magic didn't work the same on this plane. He'd tugged a bit of the magical current. Not too much. The torrent coursed wildly.

And the bowl remained inert.

"Perhaps she'll come back," Alfred stated. "With more dragons."

"She won't betray me."

"If the master insists."

The smirk in Alfred's tone ignited the heat of his doubt.

The less than subtle slam of the door exploded it. Insolent fool.

Luc's lip peeled back. He held aloft the bowl once more and chanted again, a stream of consonants guttural yet soft.

He tugged at the stream of magic he could feel nearby. Dipped his esoteric hand into it and drew a handful. He pulled it toward him, but a chunk of the stream followed.

It snapped and crackled coldly, zipping down to him, but he focused on the blood in the bowl.

A reddish glow to draw the bluish one, and threading the air around it, the green words of his breath. He kept chanting as the blue hit the red, and then the green pounced and bound it within the container.

The bowl in his grip warmed and shivered. Steam rose from the surface, and something twisted the three strands of force together.

Luc set the bowl down on the map he'd spread earlier on the table. A map with no magical properties, which was why the blood that rolled over the edge of the container ignored it. It streaked across the tabletop, seeking an edge.

It flowed down, a liquid that did not disperse. That did not soak into the rug on the floor. It oozed, its amorphous shape undulating as it made its way across the room.

He'd done it. The spell for locate.

"Alfred!" He yelled for his manservant.

"The master bellowed?" Alfred asked, appearing in the doorway.

"We must follow that blood." He jabbed a finger.

"If I might ask, sir, how does one follow a small puddle of blood?" A puddle that made it to the wall and groped its way along.

"How would I know? I've never done it before. But according to my lessons, it will take the most direct route it can."

"It has a destination, then?"

The blood reached the patio door. It probed at the door. Running along the seal at the bottom. Then up the edges.

It wanted out.

"Yes." He didn't elucidate further. Alfred had no need to know of his emasculating decision to follow Elspeth. Let him think he was doing greater work.

"I think I know how we can follow it. If the master will give me but a moment." Alfred exited the room but returned rather quickly as the blood, having not found an egress it liked via the sealed door, moved once more along the bottom edge of the wall.

Luc frowned as he noted the fireplace. Which meant a chimney.

Alfred returned with a large case that he set on a table. Unlatching it, he removed a peculiar object and set it on the table. Fiddling with it, tiny lights illuminated, and it hummed as something within its strange carcass came to life.

"What is that?" Creature. Magic. A multitude of critters harnessing their angry energy in a tiny metal box.

"It's a drone." Alfred pulled out his cellphone and aimed it at the drone thing.

"What is a drone?"

It lifted from the table with the angry buzz of a hundred bees. Luc wished he had a sword.

"It's a machine. Like a car."

"It flies without wings."

"Because it has propellers. Which, I have to admit, I don't understand. They don't seem like they should make something fly, yet…" Alfred eyed the drone, and his hand with the phone swooped. So did the device.

"You are controlling it." Luc couldn't help but sound impressed. Then scowled. "You never mentioned you could do that. You'd best not attempt to control me."

Alfred smirked. "If I controlled you, you'd never have let Miss Elspeth leave in the first place."

"This has nothing to do with Elspeth."

"Sure, it doesn't."

"Very well then, what if it does? Will you help me?"

"Would I have pulled out my drone if I weren't going to? This is technology and science at its finest." Alfred spoke with pride.

"How will this drone thing help us?"

"With this." Alfred held out the phone, and the image proved to be that of Luc's library, albeit from a lofty angle.

He was suitably impressed. "The drone has eyes."

"And an ability to lock on to something and follow it. In this case, a certain puddle."

Alfred did something on the phone, his finger

tapping and sliding. The drone bobbed low to the floor and hovered near the blood slug, which had just reached the edge of the fireplace and moved in.

The drone zipped after it. In moments, its hum disappeared. Luc stuck his head in the fireplace but could see little.

He peered over at Alfred. "Now what? We still can't follow."

"Not the way they're going, no. However, we can see where they're headed and follow in the car."

They quickly made their way to the garage, Alfred checking the phone often. Luc chose to sit alongside Alfred, fascinated by the bird's-eye view from the drone. As Alfred stated, it did follow the blood slug as it wound its way through the property.

Eyes on the phone, Alfred stated, "The blood is moving faster. Why is that?"

"It's magic." Luc shrugged. "Perhaps now that there is less obstruction, it feels its target better."

"What will you do when you catch up to Miss Elspeth?"

"I don't know." But he'd better figure it out. Because Alfred, while not within sight of either the drone or blood, managed a parallel route that allowed them to follow.

As a passenger, he had time to wonder what kind of dragon business Elspeth embarked on. Did it have some-thing to do with him? More importantly, would she return later? She'd indicated she would.

It shouldn't have excited. Yet, it did. What did that say about him? The first dragon he'd met and he couldn't avenge his mother.

Because Elspeth's innocent.

Killing her wouldn't accomplish anything. It wouldn't bring back his family or his world. It most likely wouldn't make him happy because he needed her for that.

Being with Elspeth was when he felt most free. Which proved really confusing.

"Where are we going?" he asked, noticing they'd left the more lit areas of civilization to drive upon bumpy, dark roads.

Alfred's face was lit only by the glow of the cell phone screen, giving him an eerie cast. "We've hit the countryside, but we can't go much farther. We're approaching a river."

"That won't be good for the spell," Luc muttered. Running water would wreak havoc on the binding of the spell. Or so his research had indicated. His jailors had brought him many books, filching them from the suzerain, who'd stolen them from Luc's people.

He'd learned everything he could. Memorized it. But remembering words proved to be much different from using them. Acting and touching real magic was exciting.

Luc crouched in his seat, eyes peeled on the darkness, hoping in many respects that something would dare to pounce from the shadows and provide sport.

I've been practicing my fighting moves. However, to truly test them, he needed an opponent, a real one.

"Time to go dark." Alfred tapped a red spot on the cell phone before he flicked off the beams of the car, plunging them into pure night so abrupt Luc couldn't help but blink several times as he adjusted.

"You are driving in the dark."

"We don't want them to know we're coming."

"Good point." And something Luc should have thought of. Strategy wasn't his strong suit.

Not yet, at any rate. However, every day he learned something new, absorbed knowledge, and had already begun applying it.

The car slowed to a crawl, the pitch-black unyielding, the only sound the muted purr of the engine.

The phone pinged.

Alfred stopped. "The drone is no longer moving."

"Where is it? Let us see through its eyes."

A moment later, the cell phone screen illuminated, and he saw nothing.

"Why can't I see? Are its eyes broken?"

"Broken, or something is covering the camera." Alfred frowned as he fiddled with the controls on the screen.

"The drones have predators?"

The screen flickered. Then it flashed to a green background and strange inscriptions. He'd yet to learn the human's written language.

"What does it say?" Luc asked.

"Connection lost." Alfred grimaced. "Guess we're going on foot."

"Going where?" A glance around showed nothing but layers of shadows.

"The drone might be dead, but let's see if its beacon is, too."

Luc watched as Alfred performed his own version of magic, the letters on the screen replaced by the familiar etchings of a map, the line done in a glowing shade of green. A little red dot strobed on and off amidst the green lines.

Alfred pointed. "Red is our target. Looks like we'll have to walk."

"Following your machine?" Luc eyed the phone doubtfully.

"At least it's easier to keep track of than your puddle."

Luc scowled then pointed out the obvious. "The light on your phone will act as a beacon to anyone watching."

"Which is why it will be tucked into a pocket on vibrate mode."

"Which does what?" Luc asked.

"Other than giving me a cheap thrill? Let's me know if we are heading off course."

"We? This could be dangerous. I should go alone," Luc boldly stated.

"You're right. You should."

The ease of the capitulation made Luc frown. "You're not even going to argue?" Because he'd kind of expected it. Alfred usually commented on everything Luc did.

"Traipsing through the woods with these old bones?" Alfred shook his head. "No thanks. You can go alone."

The prospect proved more daunting than he wanted to admit. Luc didn't have much experience outdoors. A few weeks here hadn't seen him venture out much. Something about the wide-open spaces intimidated him.

The world was *so* big, and he remarkably small in comparison.

Still, though, if humans could venture out with impunity, surely a demon of his lineage could, too.

"I shall do this on my own," Luc declared, grabbing the phone and shoving it into a trouser pocket.

"Do you have a weapon?"

"Of course, I do." Whether or not it would do any good remained to be seen. Luc hadn't received much training in the hand-to-hand fighting arts. What he did have was strength and determination. Also, a firearm that he'd located in a drawer by the bed. The use of it he'd seen on the television. Aim and pull the lever to fire it. Seemed simple enough.

The entire concept of sallying forth and hunting down Elspeth in the woods by himself sounded easy in theory.

Then he stepped out of the car into the darkness. The never-ending open space around him. Or did something loom in the dark? He didn't know this place. He'd never wandered it with eyes closed, fingers trailing over a stone block surface, over and over until he knew every inch of it.

He was exposed. Lost.

Times like these, he kind of missed his prison cell. There was comfort to be found in a defined space.

Only cowards hid from that which made them uncomfortable. Fear made his people bow rather than try.

Luc wasn't his father.

He strode away from the vehicle, inhaling the brisk and crisp air, redolent with living things. Green things. So many scents.

Bzzt. His thigh vibrated, startling Luc.

Wrong way. He pivoted right. Almost took a step and then whirled left. He walked, a short stride, a longer one. Normal length. No buzzing.

Easy.

Thump.

The rock surely lunged out of the ground from nowhere, grabbed him, and tossed him down. Luc pushed himself back to his feet and scowled.

This is ridiculous. He could see nothing. How was he supposed to find anything like this? He'd probably not even be able to locate his cock in this morass of darkness.

Use magic then.

The solution loomed quite obviously.

What if someone could detect it?

They would surely also hear him crashing around in the brush, making a ruckus.

The spell he needed was a simple one. One to light his way, but not with real light that anyone could see. He enchanted his eyes, placed the tips of his fingers over them as he pulled, with more confidence this time, from the river of magic so abundant in this world.

A trickle of it poured into him and pushed out through his fingers, coldly scorching the skin of his eyelids. His orbs tingled. The flow of words halted. He severed the flow and waited for the tingling to diminish before opening his eyes.

He'd not quite replaced night with day; however, he could see as if in that strange visibility before full night. Twilight, Alfred called it.

Enough for a man to thread his path through a forest. To mind the buzz in his pocket, which tickled him rather inappropriately at times.

But he enjoyed it.

As he stepped carefully, he wondered what he hoped to accomplish by spying on Elspeth. The wrongness of it nagged in his stomach like three-day-old rodent bones gnawed on to stave off hunger.

He'd come to this world for one reason, and that didn't entail caring what she did while away from him.

What if she plots?

What if her task was an innocent one?

Mother used to talk about how she and her cousins left their homes at night and collected mushrooms, scooping them into dark sacks and then hiding them in the cellars of the castle. Before the forests began to die out.

What would a dragon collect at night in the woods?

He really had to wonder as blobs of light illuminated the way up ahead. Three bobbing beams danced a few hand spans above ground. Along with it, the subtler sound of conversation.

A hum of voices. Was one of them Elspeth?

Luc crept low to the ground, doing his best to avoid detection as he realized the woods he'd trekked through ended, giving way to a lumpy vale.

Crouched behind a partially submerged boulder, its surface marked with lichen, he listened and realized he recognized Babette's voice.

"The whole place is a fucking graveyard."

"Three bodies do not—" Elspeth was cut off by a distant shout.

"I think I found two more over here."

"Okay, five bodies are a lot for one spot," Elspeth remarked. "But I can see why someone would use this place. Even in the dark, it is rather pretty."

Peeking around the boulder, Luc had to wonder what Elspeth, who stood about twenty or so paces away, considered pretty. The clearing, which stretched lopsidedly, had heavy dips and juts. With his enchanted eyes, he saw the rocks that speared from the ground, the wild grass, long and frond-like. It shared the space between the stony lumps with a mossy heather.

He noted Babette crouched at the edge of a distur-bance of soil, phone in hand, beaming out light. She pointed to something below the surface of the ground.

"Appears to be female."

"An old one. Look at how wrinkly her skin is," Elspeth remarked.

"I don't know if she was old before she died. Check out the makeup still on her skin. And the clothes. That's not the outfit of a grandma."

"Maybe she's trendy."

"Or, maybe, the person who killed her sucked the life right out of her," Babette theorized.

Guess who Luc was laying a wager on being right?

"I wonder who she is."

"This one is a dragoness."

"How can you tell?" Elspeth cocked her head. "I can't smell anything over the decomposition."

"I know she's dragon because she's wearing this locket." Babette leaned in, and a moment later, raised her hand. From it, dangled a necklace.

"What's so special about it?" Elspeth asked.

"I was asked to keep an eye open for this particular piece of jewelry."

"We have an informant?" Elspeth squealed. "How exciting."

"Less informant, more like a victim's sister. She approached me away from the Emerald Sept to tell me about her missing sibling."

"And yet Joanna assured us that no one went missing."

"Joanna lied," said Babette flatly. "Which means, I'll be paying her a visit."

Luc had no idea who this Joanna was, but he doubted she'd enjoy Babette's next social call.

"This is definitely more bodies than I expected to find."

Luc ducked behind the rock as a third person approached Elspeth and Babette. A man with a voice too smooth.

"No need to apologize. If not for you, we would have never known to look here." Elspeth sounded overly impressed.

Luc frowned.

"We're going to need some help with transport," the stranger said. "One of us should drive into town and make the arrangements."

"One of us will. Eventually. I'm curious. How did you know this field was here?"

"I got a tip."

"An anonymous one. R-i-i-ght." Luc didn't feel as special when he heard Babette using her same sarcastic tone on the stranger.

"It's no secret people have gone missing. Someone was bound to have a clue eventually." The man had a smooth reply.

"And you called us with it, not the head of the Emerald Sept."

"Because we both know they're covering it up." The man grinned. It was a nice grin.

The kind that drew an answering smile from Elspeth.

Hiding behind his rock, Luc didn't like it one bit. He scowled.

"That's a pretty bold statement."

He shrugged. "It's the truth. You see it now. They are pretending it's not happening. It's not right, which is why I came forward."

"Given you're a know-it-all, I don't suppose you know who did this?" Babette asked.

"As a matter of fact, I do. But it will sound crazy."

"Crazier than a field of bodies with the life sucked out of them?" Babette snorted. "You'd be surprised what I'd believe."

"Brace yourself. I think we have a demon in our midst."

"Demon!" Elspeth squeaked. "Those aren't real."

"They are," the male insisted.

We are too real, Luc seconded.

"You've seen one?" Babette prodded.

"Yes. I am fairly certain he lives nearby, too."

"Does he really?" Babette sounded impressed for once. "And does this demon have a name?"

Luc brushed his fingers through his hair and readied himself.

"As a matter of fact, he does. He's from the same place that dragon mage Voadicia was barfed out from. His name is…"

Lucifer stood and prepared to confront the male he finally recognized as Maedoc. A very young and unbloated version.

Elspeth's gaze widened in surprise at seeing Luc. Babette's gaze narrowed.

And Maedoc finished his sentence. "Eogan."

Chapter Eighteen

It took Elspeth a moment to grasp that the name Maedoc spoke wasn't Luc's—who was here somehow. How cute. He'd followed them. At least he'd taken her message to heart about sticking close. Good practice for later when she really needed him.

And the bodies in the ground, bodies she'd seen before in a vision, which lessened the shock, meant things were settling into the final path.

As to the enemy, Elspeth finally had a name. One she didn't recognize.

She frowned. "Who is Eogan?"

"Voadicia's closest servant," said Maedoc, the Emerald dragon snitch. He'd told them about the locket and the phone call he'd gotten from a friend of his who went hiking.

"How do you know the names of those who worked for her?" Babette asked while watching Luc who approached them, eyes blazing.

His forehead showed signs of bumps pushing at the flesh.

"I know his name because—"

"He is the brother of the dragon mage," Luc accused while pointing.

"Dragon mage? Rewind. I thought he called our killer a demon." Babette's gaze bounced to Maedoc.

"Mage, demon. Does it really matter?" Maedoc asked.

"Don't tarnish my kind with your crimes," Luc sneered as he planted his hands on his hips. "Be advised, ladies, that person styling himself as a member of a Sept is Maedoc, one of the jailors from my world. He worked with the suzerain to destroy my people."

"Only because I had no other choice." Maedoc thought he could excuse his behavior.

Luc spat on the ground at his feet. "Liar. You had a choice to die a natural death. To not prolong it by stealing the life of others. You are a perversion." Luc practically growled the words.

The man with his smooth features and thick, ebony hair offered an apologetic mien. "You mean I was. I'll have you know I've not taken a single life since my arrival here. I don't need to. I am finally free. Just like you."

Luc's lips pressed tight, and even without touching him, Elspeth could feel the anger burning inside him, saw it in how his horns pushed from his skin and his voice dropped a few octaves.

"Foul dragon," Luc spat. "We are nothing alike. While I starved in a cell, you were fat and bloated topside. You were never locked away. Never forced to suck at the moisture in the cracks of blocks. Never had to wonder if the next time you woke would be your last."

Maedoc sneered. "Show a little gratitude. I kept you safe. The suzerain would have eaten you alive. Even Eogan wanted to have a piece of you. I convinced him not to."

"Only so you could steal more secrets. More magic." Luc's voice deepened further, and his skin took on a grayish cast.

"You were learning, too."

"Because I had no choice." The words spat out of Luc, and the tips of his fingers shot longer and became clawed.

"Am I understanding this correctly?" Elspeth interrupted, well-aware that Luc seethed, his inner demon pushing at his surface. "This guy was one of your jailors. One of the people directly responsible for the extinction of your race. The death of your parents."

"Yes." His eyes blazed even brighter, and his horns pushed through the skin of his forehead and kept pushing, curling a bit at the end.

Almost there…

Elspeth kept stoking his anger. "Seems like Maedoc is one of the reasons you have nothing left."

"Hey, hold on," snapped the man. "What are you doing?"

Luc's gaze turned red as he looked upon Maedoc. "You did nothing to save us." The words emerged hot and gruff. The shirt at his back tented as if wings might be sprouting at his back.

"I kept your ass alive," Maedoc argued. "I freed you."

"You killed my mother." Luc could barely get the syllables to roll off his tongue.

"He did," Elspeth whispered. "When your mother spoke of revenge, this was who she meant."

"Yesss." The word had a sibilant hiss to it.

Maedoc's gaze narrowed. "I know not what game you play, little girl, but I would advise you keep your demon under control."

"Or what?" purred Babette, jumping in to sass. "Afraid now that Luc's not in a cage anymore he might be able to whoop your ass?"

"He's but a baby when it comes to fighting," Maedoc declared, cupping his hands and showcasing a glowing orb. "With just this, I could extinguish you where you stand. I can even put the demon to sleep with just a word. Azzzreyoth."

Luc crumpled, and his features smoothed. All hint of demon gone.

"What's your end game?" Babette asked, unimpressed by the ball of magic. Whereas Elspeth bit her tongue before she crooned, "Ooh, pretty light." Auntie Sylvie often muttered that Elspeth had a hint of squirrel somewhere in her bloodline.

"Does a man need a reason to do the right thing and ensure justice?" Maedoc said, holding the light ball in one hand while slapping his free hand on his chest in an aggrieved pose.

"I'd say you need a reason. Why are you ratting on your dragon brother?" Babette shook her head. "That is so not cool."

Maedoc might act big and tough, but he had an annoying slickness to him, the kind that screamed he liked to cheat. And boast.

He was also a snitch.

"Now that we've all escaped Hell, we have the

option of a second chance. But I won't get that if I can't get the killing to stop."

What kind of brother ratted out his own? Having been the accomplice more than once for the family, Elspeth had vowed to never tell anyone where she buried the bodies.

"And your brother is the killer?" Babette asked him directly.

"Yes."

Which caused Elspeth to frown. She couldn't read truth or lie in this. As a matter of fact, she could read nothing at all from the man.

"Is he also part of the Emerald Sept like you?"

"Yes. It's how he got involved with Joanna. He's made her certain promises. In return, she's removed some of the more annoying and useless members of her Sept and covered it up."

"She offered up her own people?" Even Babette sounded shocked.

Elspeth had seen too much in her visions to be shocked by anything anyone could do.

"Joanna had no choice but to comply after Eogan captured her. As part of the terms of her release, she was expected to facilitate some of his meals."

Elspeth's stomach turned. "He ate them."

"He ate their life force," Luc said softly, the sleep spell not having kept him down for long. He struggled to his feet, no sign of the demon rising. But Elspeth knew it was there. It just needed the right incentive to come out.

Count on Babette to ask the tough questions. "If you and your bro both came from Hell, how come your brother is eating people and you aren't?"

"I am not driven as he is to feed."

Luc shook his head. "It's more than that. Eogan does it because he enjoys it."

"Enjoys killing people?" Elspeth asked. "That does seem wrong even if he's doing it to survive."

"But he doesn't need it." Luc's words held a mocking lilt. "Because the sickening thing about the magic to take someone's life is it's not cumulative. Taking a large amount of someone's life at once isn't necessary. You can't keep extending by imbibing over and over. The essence stolen moves linearly."

"Which means what?" Babette asked. "In English."

Maedoc spread his hands. "What he's saying is we didn't have to kill everything. While it might have seemed like we needed to in order to keep extending our lives, the fact of the matter was that we would only live as long as what we stole from our last host."

"The theft only gave you their lifespan? It couldn't be stacked?"

"Correct. We could go years between feedings if we wanted. And at first, we did. It's why it took centuries before we ran out. However, the magic, the euphoria of immortality…" Maedoc's eyes closed, and he inhaled deeply. "Ambrosia. We bloated ourselves on life. We ate because we couldn't control our appetites."

Luc sneered. "You talk as if the ingesting of my people was a large meal and you got indigestion. You committed genocide because it felt good." Luc's blazing gaze turned her way, his features taking on an alien cast with his cheekbones sharper than usual and his skin turning dark. The demon within hadn't sunk far.

"It did feel good," Maedoc admitted. "Incredibly delicious. Did you expect me to lie about it? There's a reason some of us acted the way we did. The taking of life, the imbibing of it…" Maedoc's lips curved, and he took a deep breath. "It's…well, more divine that you can imagine. Orgasmic even." Maedoc held Elspeth's gaze as he said the last bit.

Luc rumbled, a bestial growl that saw Elspeth worriedly taking a step closer.

Babette, however, kept plowing ahead. "What you're saying is that your brother, Eogan, is killing these women because he wants to get high."

"He is addicted. Which is why he must be stopped. Just like we must trap the demon in our midst." Maedoc fixed Luc with a stare. "My brother isn't the only guilty one."

"He lies. I don't indulge in perversion."

"You should try sometime, demon spawn." Maedoc grinned. "Maybe if you're a good demon, I'll show you some of my favorite positions."

"What are you talking about?"

For a moment, Elspeth got a disturbing vision of her and Luc in chains. Naked. But not alone.

"Lucky for you, I brought some items from the other side. One especially guaranteed to tame a demon."

Tame Luc? Elspeth frowned as Maedoc withdrew a pair of shackles from his satchel. Another reason to dislike him. His satchel was much nicer than hers. But those handcuffs he pulled from them gave her the shivers. She knew that metal.

Babette barked, "What are those? Why is it making me pimple worse than the time I did a polar dip?"

"Because this is dracinore. A metal from Hell. It stops the demon from changing."

Luc spat, "It is how Voadicia and the others subjugated my people."

"Don't blame us for using the tools at hand. The stuff was lying around everywhere. We simply harnessed it." Maedoc acted as if this were normal.

Even Elspeth was hard-pressed to find a positive spin. "Why do you have it? It is forbidden." Because it was the metal the dragon mages smuggled into this dimension that caused the dragons to lose the war against humans. It also saw their numbers plummeting, sending them into hiding from the hunters, trying to rebuild their numbers. Centuries later, humanity knew about them again. And this time, they were even more numerous, as well as armed.

Imagine if a certain military-geared government got their hands on this metal? She could see a future where dragons were slaves.

Luc seethed, his bulking body tense. "Try and put those on and see what happens."

"No one is handcuffing anyone. Unless there's a bed involved." Make love, not anything else, was Elspeth's motto.

Maedoc twirled them on his finger. "We must trap him. He's a demon."

"Yup. He is. And according to your own words, a victim of dragon mages. Which makes us look bad. The PR folk won't like that at all. There will probably be reparations involved and complicated repayment schemes." Elspeth was so proud of Babette's grown-up reasoning.

Maedoc pursed his lips. "Are you taking the side of a demon over a dragon?"

"I am taking the side of a guy I know over you," Elspeth corrected. "I don't like you." Mostly because she couldn't see his face in any of her futures. Yet, he obviously would play a role. He was too evil not to.

"Don't like me?" Maedoc's lips rounded. "Impossible."

"Guess again, douchenozzle. I don't like you either," Babette confided.

"Your hatred is to be expected. It's why the suzerain seduced you in a feminine shape." Maedoc casually admitted that Babette had been led astray on purpose.

Her bestie took it with a stoic face and clenched fists. "I am going to bend you so far you're going to have your head shoved up your ass," she promised with a smile.

"Now, Babsy, let's not be hasty. No one has to get hurt today." She held out soothing hands.

"Way to ruin everyone's fun," Babette growled. "Ever think a girl is intentionally trying to start a fight?"

"Fighting doesn't solve anything."

"Now you sound like my father," Luc grumbled.

"This entire conversation is boring. As is your interest in the demon. Did he seduce you? Is that why you would prefer to support him over me?" Maedoc affected effrontery. Clutching his chest melodramatically.

"I wish he'd seduce me. But he's too polite for that." Elspeth finally found a reason to roll her eyes.

"I won't be polite anymore," Luc muttered.

I should be so lucky.

Elspeth moved closer to Maedoc, who still dangled those cuffs. "You know, I am really beginning to wonder about your motives. Why did you call us? Because it was you, not some anonymous tipster, right?"

"It is kind of funky, especially since you're claiming that you kicked the habit of eating people's souls,"

Babette remarked. "Seems interesting you can do it that easily when your brother couldn't."

"Never said it was easy." Maedoc tucked the cuffs away, and his chin dropped as he regarded them from behind a long hank of dark hair. Amidst the strands, his eyes glowed red. "And, sometimes, I might have a wee lapse."

Mind you, Elspeth had not met many dragon mages, Maedoc being the first, actually—rumor said Samael might be one, too, but she liked him. Despite her lack of experience, she was gonna bet that, since no one else sported red eyes, it probably meant something.

What was a dragon mage's secret weapon?

Anything he can imagine.

The very idea was why she knew to throw herself at Luc when Maedoc's hand rose and a fireball launched from it.

"You double crossing bastard," Babette screeched. "I'm going to fuck—*trill. Tweet.*" A transformed Babs fluted the things she'd do to Maedoc. None of them possible without bones breaking.

Trusting that Babette could take care of herself for just a minute, Elspeth turned her head to better talk to Luc, given she lay plastered atop him—a living shield.

"Hi, good-looking. What's cooking?"

He squinted up. "While new at relations with the opposite sex, I am fairly certain you've emasculated me. Possibly beyond repair."

"Did I crush your balls?" She squirmed and almost cheered as she felt something stirring. His equipment seemed to be in working order.

"I am talking of my pride. Why did you throw yourself on me?"

"To protect you."

"Because you think I'm weak." His lips pulled down.

"No, because I saw the danger and acted."

"Because I am vastly inexperienced."

"For now. But that will change. You can learn."

"I can't learn if you keep saving me."

"Would you have preferred I let you be a victim of that fireball?"

"Yes."

"You are just like every dumb guy I've ever met then." She sighed. Kind of disappointed.

"Thank you."

"What?" She blinked on account of her ears not working.

"I said thank you because you are correct. The emasculating encounter quite possibly saved my life. It is a reminder that I must be more vigilant and faster so that I might save you in the future."

She blinked again because jumping jellybeans on a griddle, her ears still weren't darned working.

"Save me? But I'm a dragon." He hated her kind.

A true dilemma, given her fascination with him. She kept staring at him as Babette trilled something rude and silver dust lifted into the air. Babette was still playing with Maedoc, who laughed.

"Is that the best you can do, sweetheart? I expected more out of you. Maybe I won't make you my lunch for a while."

Blart. That was definitely a rude bugle.

It almost hid Luc's words. "I'd save you because I can't help myself. You are…"

He didn't finish his sentence. He didn't have to because she suddenly saw it, a possible future that flashed in the blink of an eye, a lightning-quick peek at what could be if she made the right choices.

And if she failed and turned down the wrong fork? She'd already seen how she would die. Knew it down to the ruby-red rockabilly dress in her closet with the glittering Dorothy shoes.

Without her drugs to shield her, the vision shook her like a lone loose leaf in a tempest. She collapsed, her body turning into a boneless jelly mess. Arms caught her, swept her high.

Voices spoke, buzzing high and far away. The effort to truly listen was too much. She preferred to snuggle against her warm rock.

The rock would keep her safe.

In her quiet space, nobody spoke, nobody listened. She might have floated away if the rock hadn't remained constant.

He even tucked her into a bed, the sheets soft. He thought he could leave.

A whimper solved that.

He cradled her body against his, anchoring her to this reality and not the madness of her dreams. Only in the cocoon of his arms did she finally allow herself to truly shut down her mind.

When she next woke, the sun was shining, she was feeling great, and Luc was in bed.

With her.

It was only right that she straddle him, grab his hands, and pin them over his head before he could move, and sing, "Oh, what a beautiful morning."

Chapter Nineteen

S he dared to call it beautiful!

Luc glared at Elspeth. "You."

"Yes, it's me. And?" She cocked her head.

The cuteness did nothing to quell his anger. "You almost died."

"You mean that fainting spell?" She blew a noise through her lips. "Nope. Nothing deadly about it. I had a vision. A whopper of one. Happens when I go off my meds for too long."

"You mean this has occurred in the past? But you lost consciousness." The fact still had the capacity to chill him. How frightening to see how she shook, trembled, and drooled.

All he could do was cradle her, his magic of healing dispersing each time he called it. It could find nothing to mend. What ailed her was of the mind, not the body.

A flash of silver had caught his eye, and he had looked up to see Babette soaring in the sky, her bugling cry a challenge. Yet Maedoc was nowhere to be seen.

The dragon mage had disappeared. Probably off to kill more people.

Luc cared not a whit about anyone else. He called Babette. "Something is ailing Elspeth. She fainted."

Alighting in a gleam of silver scales, Babette cocked her head and trilled.

While her accent was quite American, he still understood the dragon-speak. He shook his head. "What if she needs more than sleep? On your television, they would take her to a hospital."

That caused Babette to shift, and him to avert his gaze. "You can't take a dragon to a human hospital. Especially not one having a fit. What if she accidentally changes?"

"What if she dies because we lack the proper medicine?" It'd happened in the dungeons. Common ailments that they once could cure, felling them. Making them an earlier victim to the suzerain.

"Then we know a field to bury her in."

He glared hotly at Babette. "I thought she was your family."

"She is. Which is how I know she's tough."

"Even the toughest sometimes require nurturing. She is coming home with me since you refuse to care for her."

"What's watching going to do? Either she dies, or she doesn't."

At that point, he'd swept Elspeth into his arms. Alfred remained parked by the side of the road. He sat behind the wheel, head tilted back, snoring.

During the ride home, while Babette regaled Alfred in the front, Luc sat in the back with Elspeth on his lap. Then he'd ended up in bed with her because she mewled, as if lost and scared. It drew out the protective side of him. He cradled her body with his own. Giving his warmth. Wondering what she'd seen.

Questioning what had happened to him.

And he wasn't just talking about his evolving feelings for this woman and dragons in general.

He'd not forgotten how he'd almost managed *the change* in the field. He'd felt that fluttering second half of himself pulsing in his breast. Pushing to get out.

For a moment, it almost did. The idea of losing control, losing himself, made him glad that it had failed, even as he feared it trying again.

The wildness was awake inside him. Pulsing in his veins. Making him feel…alive.

So much so, that he wanted to act.

Especially now.

Elspeth crouched over him, brighter than the sun's rays streaming through the windows. He'd finally started to leave the fabric panels pulled open when he realized that a light so bright wouldn't crisp him to a strip of bacon. Now that brilliance illuminated her, more luminescent than any jewel.

He might not be a dragon, but in that moment, he coveted her. Wanted her all to himself. Yet, how would that work? He had little to offer. He commanded no legions. He couldn't even protect her.

At this point, she was stronger than he. Perhaps it might have bothered another male. He'd seen some of the posturings on the screen and when he went out. But he'd grown up in a society based on mutual respect. Male or female, worth was based on intelligence and merit and skill.

Being intelligent meant knowing when to ask for help.

"Can I ask you something?" Luc said as she beamed down at him.

She wet her lips, a quick cock-hardening sweep of a pink tip over a full mouth. "Yes. Ask me." She squirmed over him.

"Can you teach me to fight?"

"You want me to get physical with you?" Her lips quirked, and her eyes sparkled. She placed her hands on his chest and leaned forward, at the same time grinding down with her hips.

He lost all the blood to his brain when her lips came close enough that the heat of her words branded his skin.

"I'll teach you. For a kiss."

A price?

Then again, not really a price, more like an unexpected boon. Lessons in sparring and…

He gripped her and pulled her close, removing the space between them. The mash of lips a hard clash.

Clumsy idiot.

He tried to relax, but his muscles refused to obey. He remained tense.

He was totally ruining this.

Failing.

She would totally hate—

Her lips slanted over his, and her hands cupped his jaw. She feathered light embraces over his mouth before tugging his lower lip.

That caused a tremble to go through him.

She pulled his lip again, the tiny bite of her teeth something he felt right down to his cock.

Then she let go and pulled away.

He struggled to understand. His poor erection strained, screaming for relief.

But his relief was strutting to the door.

"Where are you going?" he asked.

"Breakfast, then training. Which means, get your sexy ass out of bed."

"What if I changed my mind about the lessons and said you should return to bed?"

She cast him a saucy smirk over her shoulder. "I'll come back and even share a shower if you pin me before the day is done."

"I'm not interested in winning sexual favor."

"Says the guy who wants me back in bed." Elspeth leaned against the doorjamb, looking adorably tousled from sleep.

"I never claimed I didn't want you. I very much do. But I want it to happen because it's supposed to. Not on account of a wager."

"You have morals."

He wanted to sneer at the idea. His father had had morals, and look where it had gotten him and the rest.

It occurred to him more and more that perhaps the right choice was to adopt some of his father's ideals and Mother's proud spirit. Could he achieve a balance?

"We should find Alfred and see what he's prepared."

"The king of dodge." She smiled with the cryptic remark before pivoting to head out the door, her hips a sashaying sway away from getting tossed back on the bed.

She moved fast. Too fast. He emerged from his room to find her doing handsprings down the hall. She hit the top of the stairs, held the newel post two-handed, legs above her, her strength incredible.

Tall, fit…*mine…*

She swung down, and for a moment, he held his breath. She caught the railing and with a hollered, "See you at the bottom," slid down.

He raced down the hall and braked at the last moment, teetering at the top. Peering down in time to see Elspeth speeding toward the bottom newel post and yet, before she hit it, flipping off and hitting the floor in a solid, two-footed stance.

Show-off. She made it look so easy.

He recognized the jealousy for what it was and overcame it. Clapped instead. "That was excellent."

"You try it," she hollered.

Him, ride a railing? How utterly undignified.

"Don't be scared."

Did she impugn his manhood? This was now a matter of honor.

He eyed the contraption and ignored the distance between where he stood and the floor far below. He grabbed hold of the rail and swung himself onto it.

A little bit hard. He immediately swung all the way over, hard enough that he snapped his grip on the rail and began to drop.

The realization that he'd die if he hit the floor below wrong had him thrusting out a hand and quickly shouting out the words to a spell. The magical lasso lashed itself to the rail, and his descent abruptly halted, sending him swinging on his magical rope.

He twisted his body before he hit a wall and managed to push off in the other direction while trying to lengthen the magical strand.

Someone sang about a spider man. Which he ignored. If there were spiders, he'd have Alfred deal with them.

Eventually, Luc hit the floor, running a few steps to regain his balance while Elspeth clapped.

"Bravo. That looked fun. Can you teach me to do it?"

"It was magic."

Her nose scrunched. "Which means, no. Can you take a passenger?"

Could he handle more weight on his magical rope? He didn't know. Just like he didn't know how he'd reacted that quickly.

"Perhaps I'll let you find out later."

It might depend on how badly things went during their lesson after breakfast.

Alfred wasn't to be found in the kitchen. However, a large, covered tray and a note claiming he'd gone to run errands were.

Luc chewed slowly at the flaky roll she had called some fancy name and listened as she babbled.

Elspeth enjoyed talking, and he liked listening. She had a certain joy about her that radiated in everything she did.

She noticed him staring. "Do I have something stuck in my teeth?" She smiled widely.

"No."

"Then why are you ogling me like that?"

"Because you're beautiful."

Sunshine beamed from her face. "Thank you. You're pretty, too."

With such an opening, he blurted, "We should return to my chambers."

"Oh, no you don't. You asked me to teach you how to fight, and I am a woman of my word."

And she kept it, giving him no quarter as she taught him the basics of hand-to-hand combat. Most of it he picked up quickly, his study of the television having given him an idea of the movements. Still, implementing proved trickier than expected. She was so very fast.

When she swept him to the mat, again, for the umpteenth—no one was counting—time, he couldn't help a wry grin.

"I might not be ready to rule the world."

"A little more practice," she agreed, lying atop him, a light sheen of sweat slicking her skin. Her hair was held back with a strip of fabric, but a few wispy curls strayed to frame her face.

If this was practice, give him more.

She squirmed atop him. "I think we're done for the day."

But he'd not yet pinned her. She was too quick. What if he caught her off guard?

He kissed her, a sudden embrace met with a heated gasp. Elspeth didn't pull away. She melted into him, her lips embracing his with a fierce hunger. Her body molded to his. It made it easy for him to put his arms around her, hold her tight, and then...

Flip. She lay under. He lay over. The kiss continued, and he pressed against her. Hard and aching.

He whispered against her lips. "I pinned you."

Her hot reply? "I know. I think I promised you a shower."

"Later." He didn't want this kiss to end.

She held tightly to him, her lips melded to his, their

breaths mixed and hot. Her legs parted, allowing him to nestle more fully between them. But their clothing remained in the way.

It didn't stop him from grinding against her, his need great. The ache unbearable.

"Undress me," she whispered in between nips of his mouth. "Let's do it right here, right now."

On the floor?

He might have argued more, but she tugged at his shirt. He lifted enough to strip it, and she ran her fingers over his flesh, leaving paths of fire in their wake.

His attempt to denude her didn't fare as well. His hands became frantic and clumsy.

She laughed as she helped him. "It's okay. We have time."

Perhaps she could slow down, but he couldn't. He'd waited so long. So long to be this close to a woman. To find someone he could be intimate with.

She wore a brassiere over her breasts, the fabric both covering and revealing. He gripped it on the sides and tore it. Having seen enough movies to know it would be easier than wrestling with it.

It revealed her in all her naked splendor. This time, he didn't look away.

He stared. She was utterly perfect, from her smooth skin, her toned muscles, to her breasts tipped in pink.

Looks good enough to eat.

With their shirts gone, crushing himself against her proved very different.

Skin-to-skin contact. It caused him to draw a deep, shuddering breath. Then another as her nipples shriveled to hard points that pressed into his chest. The friction proved pleasurable. He couldn't help but rub himself over and over against her. He hardness of him pressing and grinding against the vee of her thighs. Her lips latched hotly to his, and their tongues… Their tongues twined, drawing groan after groan.

The pressure in him built.

He drew close. Too close. He'd yet to remove her pants or his.

To gain some measure of control, he reared, tearing himself away from her tempting skin. Only she reached forward and raked his bare chest with her nails

"I—I—" His head fell back, and his hips jerked as he came.

Chapter Twenty

Elspeth blinked. Then smiled even as Luc groaned and rolled away from her.

"Where are you going?" she exclaimed.

"To bury myself in a hole since I'm about to die from shame," he grumbled, refusing to look at her.

"What shame?"

He turned his head enough to shoot her a dark glare. "We are not discussing this."

"I don't see what the problem is. I'm rather honored by it all."

"Honored?" He rose to his feet, hands dropped to cover the wet stain on his pants. "You didn't achieve pleasure. I was selfish."

"You lost control. Which is the sexiest thing a man has ever done for or with me." She beamed at him.

"But you didn't achieve pleasure. I failed."

"Only if we're done. Are we done? Or will you join me in a shower?" She rose to her feet, noting how his gaze hotly followed the sway of her breasts.

"What if it happens again?"

"Then the third time is the charm."

Emotions rippled across his face: shame, hope, eagerness, hesitation…

"I fear I should warn you, I might not be the most adept of lovers."

"It's okay if you don't have much experience."

Watching him meant seeing the rising tide of red in his cheeks.

"I have no experience." He cleared his throat. "By the time I came of age, it was only my mother and me. We would never have committed that cardinal sin. And after, I only had my jailors. I would have died before I let them touch me."

"Everyone starts out a virgin."

"Are you?" he asked.

A soft smile graced her lips as she nodded. "Yes." Not for lack of trying. "Which means this will be a learning adventure for us both. So long as we stay away from those heated massage oils." That didn't end well.

She held out her hand.

"You still want to be with me?" He sounded surprised.

She nodded. "Do you?" They'd not known each other for very long. He'd only recently escaped. His psyche was still adapting to all the changes he'd gone through. But biggest of all, she knew how he struggled with the vengeance he thought he wanted and the affection and friendship she knew he needed.

They both needed this. She had already seen that he was the only man strong enough to handle her. To not be daunted by her power. Who wouldn't be crushed by her passion.

When he approached and ignored her hand to draw

her close, she couldn't help the happy burst within her. He'd chosen her over revenge.

Little did he know, she'd choose him over anything.

Their lips melded, a hard clash of mouths and teeth. There was nothing gentle about their kiss. Nothing elegant either.

Pure.

Unadulterated.

Passion.

She held tightly to his shoulders and lifted her legs to wrap around his waist.

Luc didn't even grunt at the added weight. Simply took that as an invitation to cup her ass cheeks.

"Let's have that shower," she whispered against his neck before licking it.

Lucky for them, the basement gym in the castle—a converted dungeon that mixed medieval stone with modern convenience—had a huge bathroom. A room— probably an old cell—equipped with a tiny frosted window high on the wall, offered showerheads on a few of the surfaces. Knobs sat below each.

"Which one?" he asked.

"Turn them all on," she replied. "Let's steam this place up."

She sucked at his ear as he carried her from tap to tap, yanking the knobs and turning them, dodging out of the way of the cold water that first shot out.

At the last knob he didn't move, and he let the cold spray strike their bodies.

She gasped and tightened her grip on him.

His fingers dug deeper as the fabric to her pants became soaked.

"You set me afire," he murmured, taking a page from her book and nuzzling her neck.

"It's because we're made for each other." They were soul mates.

She'd seen it.

"I burn for you." He shoved her back against the shower wall, the old stone blocks smoothed by time, yet chilly against her skin. Her new position freed his hands.

He threaded one through her hair, cradling her head. He tugged, and she tilted her face, exposing her neck to him.

His lips grazed the skin. He whispered, "You make me forget my promises."

Awash in pleasure, she replied, "I would do anything for you." Love, kill, betray. He was her dracinore. Her weakness.

Some would argue that she barely knew the man, but how could she say that? In her visions, she'd experienced a thousand different lifetimes with him. She remembered none clearly. They jumbled together in her mind, but there was one thing they all had in common.

"Luc." She breathed his name and moaned as his lips left her neck for the bounty of her breasts. For a girl her height, she didn't have the largest ones. Not by far. She exercised too much for that. But Luc didn't seem to mind. He nuzzled her breasts, rubbed his bristly jawline against them as the water, now hot, sluiced over them.

When he finally stopped teasing to place his mouth over a tip, she arched and cried out.

He paused.

"Keep going."

With a happy hum, he played again, sucking softly at

first but, with encouragement, tugging hard at her nipple—the pulls tugging between her legs.

Speaking of which, her damned wet pants chafed.

"Take these off me." She looped her fingers into the waistband, shoving at them.

It took a few fumbles before they were nude.

She took a moment to admire the long and thick jut of his cock before he clasped her tightly to him once more. Full-body contact.

Her pussy quivered. She might have come a little.

The kiss was even fiercer than before. Their tongues dueled wetly.

His hands grabbed hold of her and lifted, with no help from her. He wasn't as gentle when her back slammed into the wall.

Damn did she like it.

She wrapped her legs around his shank and kept him close, rubbing her heated core against his lower belly. Feeling the hot throb of his dick below her butt.

"Rub it against me," she ordered. Being a virgin didn't mean she didn't know what she wanted.

I've experienced this in my dreams.

Yet they hadn't prepared her for the electrical charge of it.

Elspeth rarely lost control. She couldn't. No one could handle it. *She* could barely handle it.

But Luc could. He wanted all of her. No pretense, and no holding back.

The tip of him rubbed against the petals of her sex. She shuddered and moaned, her fingers digging into the flesh of his shoulders. Those lovely, broad shoulders.

He slicked it back and forth, drawing shivers and groans and tightening desperation.

"Now, Luc. I need you."

Needed him so damned much.

The head of him paused at the opening of her sex.

He held off, despite the tension thrumming in him.

"Why are you stopping?" she asked, the hot breath against his ear wringing a fine tremor in his frame.

"I'm not in control."

"And?" She licked the outer part of his ear. "Neither am I. This will either end well or it won't. But I've seen the future, and I'm wagering on explosive." She bit the lobe, and his hips jerked.

He slid into her.

Just a bit. It stole her breath.

He's big.

It will fit.

He pushed a little deeper, stretching her.

What if it doesn't?

He didn't move. He didn't speak. He didn't have to. She knew why he froze.

He didn't want to hurt her.

This demon, abused and abandoned, alone for a long time, worried about her.

She cupped his face and met his gaze. "Don't be afraid. I'm not. This is our destiny."

She didn't give him a soft kiss. She bit him. Grabbed that lower lip of his and nipped it hard enough to draw blood.

She sucked, and he bucked, his hips grinding forward, taking their innocence in one swift move.

A moment that surely made the world tremble. Her existence was certainly rocked.

He fit within her perfectly. Their bodies moving in

synchronicity. The bond between them forming with the shedding of blood.

It further strengthened when they kissed.

And when they came, an explosion intent enough to steal her breath, she felt his aura. Hard and cold, yet it went well with her warm persona, a shield against the ugly beyond it.

When she finally caught her breath enough to realize that they were still in the shower turning into shriveled prunes, she smiled and nuzzled his skin.

And what did she have to say about this monumental moment in her life?

"That was epic."

The entire night proved to be one enjoyable thing after another. As older virgins, they had a lot of pent-up frustration to deal with.

The man was a beast. And she was… *In love.*

But love didn't mean shirking her duty to the Sept— and it wouldn't help her avoid what was coming.

Time to get moving.

The next morning, Elspeth rose from the bed. She smiled down at Luc, who snored softly amidst the tangled sheets. She brushed back his hair and enjoyed one last touch, one last look.

She left her clothes on the floor. Left everything behind as she exited his room and padded to a guest room across from it. Far enough from him that she could shower and do her toilette duties.

She performed those tasks quickly. She'd lingered longer than she should have in bed.

At least she'd had the forethought to have her luggage delivered to his place, which meant she could put clean clothes in this room, preparation for later. Say thank you to her vision advantage. Seeing herself in a few grubby, I-slept-in-those clothes in dreams helped make sure she controlled at least something.

Exiting the bedroom, she paused for a moment, staring at the door behind which Luc still slept. Despite the night they'd spent making it clear how she felt, it occurred to her before leaving that she should write him a note.

It took but a moment to jot something and slide it under his door.

Then, off to destiny. Alone. Which was kind of scary, but she had to do this. Had to leave Luc for him to find himself. He wouldn't understand her choice. He wasn't supposed to. But, hopefully, he would become what he had to in time to save her because she neared that damned fork. The biggest stumble in her life's path.

Of late, she didn't see anything beyond it. Not a good omen.

Arriving downstairs, she caught Alfred in the kitchen tucking away his cell phone. He looked rather distressed.

Entering, she noted some delivery bags and food partially placed on plates. Here she'd thought dear Alfred did all the cooking himself. Sly man.

She wandered closed enough to snare a piece of crisp bacon and dipped it in an open pitcher of syrup.

Only as the sugar and salt hit her tongue did she ask, "Did someone accuse the butler of doing it?"

"Not quite. Rather the master. A friend of mine was calling to warn me the coppers have a warrant to search the castle."

"What for?"

"Someone tipped them off about the bodies in the field."

"You know about the bodies?" she asked, grabbing a croissant and shredding it to eat it.

"I was the one driving the master that night."

"Which reminds me. We never did ask how you found us."

"A spell by the master. I drove since it led him a fair distance."

"You're awfully efficient, Alfred. I'm going to enjoy having you as a butler. You just wait, next Halloween, guess what we'll dress up as?"

Alfred didn't look amused. It was utterly perfect.

"I have to leave," he remarked.

"Where are you going? Need a hand?"

"As a matter of fact, I do. Groceries again. You know how heavy those are." Alfred rubbed his lower back while Elspeth snared a danish.

"Sure thing. Let's go now so we can return before Luc wakes up."

Alfred led the way to a lovely town car. Slick and black, the interior very clean with a hint of perfume.

Not her perfume.

"Is this the car Luc likes using?" she asked, unable to help herself from asking the jealous query. She ran a hand over the smooth paint heading for the passenger side.

"No. This is the one I prefer. It's got some nice features for the driver. Get in the back, and I'll show you some of the perks."

Intrigued, she clambered into the back seat. The perfume scent stronger than before with something else.

Something oddly familiar.

Click.

The door locked.

Whir. A sheet of glass rose forming a wall to separate the front and back. *Hiss.*

Gas vapors emerged from some vents while, from a speaker, she heard Alfred say, "Dumb blonde. You should have stayed in bed with your demon lover."

No, thank you. She'd seen that future. It didn't go well for anyone.

Chapter Twenty-One

Stretching in bed, Luc found himself smiling. He had plenty to grin about after last night.

A virgin no more.

He had one sexy female to thank for that. Speaking of whom, he rolled over in bed and realized that she wasn't beside him.

Probably off hunting down some food. The woman had a healthy appetite. She possessed gusto for many things, including life.

And me.

Rising from the bed, he reveled in the cool air brushing his nude skin. In the dungeons, the heat from the molten lava running below the ground's surface made it warmer below than above.

He'd never even imagined what something chilly would feel like and found himself eager to experience his first snow.

As a matter of fact, Luc found himself eager for a lot of things now. His life was truly about to begin. Especially since, now that he'd let go of some of his anger, he could see a future.

One with Elspeth.

He slid on a pair of pants and a shirt. Alfred frowned when he went about half dressed. The old man was probably jealous of his much younger body.

Although, truth be told, Luc hoped he appeared half as fit as Alfred at that age. His own father had been much frailer.

As he headed toward the bedroom door, he noticed a slip of paper on the floor. A scrap hastily scribbled on in red.

A note he couldn't read. But he could guess at the contents.

The fool woman! What had she done? Because he had no doubt she'd hared off, probably acting on some vision.

And she didn't expect to return.

Unacceptable. They were tied together. *She and I, forever.* The things she did would affect him. He'd die without her, mostly because he'd lay waste to the world until it killed him. He'd lost everything else in his life. He couldn't lose her, too.

Exiting the bedroom, he didn't hear a sound. Most definitely not Elspeth's warming laughter. She was always happy. He understood better now that she used it as a defense mechanism against the dark things she saw. He admired her all the more for not letting despair be her constant companion.

In the face of adversity, she fought. She feared nothing. Not even the hauntings of her own mind.

The scent of her hovered. Strong, especially across the hall. A quick glance through the bedroom showed her passage. An old trail. He returned to the hall and strode to the staircase.

The treads were a gleaming wood. Nothing like the stone block steps in the castle he'd grown up in. The bannister, the same one he'd attempted to slide down yesterday, taunted. He eyed the railing. He could do this. It just required a little balance—and maybe a touch of magic.

This time, when he grabbed the rail, he used a cushion of magic to keep him from tilting. It was getting easier to allow the power to fill him up.

The dungeons never gave him much of a chance to do anything; the very ore in the stone created a dampening effect on his spells. Those he and his mother managed were but pale imitations.

Nothing fettered him now. He could truly manipulate the esoteric forces, and he used them, of all things, to have fun.

Because that was what sliding down quickly on a thin piece of wood entailed. Adrenalized pleasure.

An exuberant, "Yaaaaay," emerged from him as he soared.

He then lost all breath as he slammed into the newel post at the bottom.

Balls first.

Kill him now. The pain proved intense.

He slumped off the rail, losing hold of his magic cushion, and hit the floor, groaning.

He really hoped that Elspeth wouldn't choose this moment to witness his discomposure.

As he writhed, he, at the very least, expected his nosy manservant, Alfred, to appear and mock him.

However, instead, he got treated to Babette uttering a somber, "Get off the floor so I can kick your ass."

Rolling over, he peered up at her with one eye—all he could manage as the pain radiated through him. A throb that screamed that he'd broken his cock.

The horror.

There was no sympathy or humor in Babette's gaze. It brought a chill. He pushed up to an elbow and asked, "What's wrong?"

Rather than reply, she posed her own question. "Where's Elspeth?"

"I don't know. I woke to find her gone." He didn't yet mention the note. Not with the sorrow and anger in Babette's gaze. "Did you check to see if she's in the kitchen with Alfred?"

Babette shook her head. "You already know she isn't. Where is she? Is she still in the castle?"

"I don't know." The simple truth.

"You can stop it, dude. We know you're the one who's been kidnapping the women."

His hand slashed through the air, magical motes visible only to him clinging in preparation. "I have no idea what you're talking about. I've taken no women."

"Liar," Babette spat. "The evidence all leads back to this castle."

"Impossible, and have you so soon forgotten? Maedoc already told you it was his brother."

"Are you his brother?"

The very idea had him gaping. Luc rose to his feet and retorted, quite indignantly, "Most certainly not."

"Then Maedoc lied. Or maybe he truly thought his sibling was to blame. But the clues tell a different story, one that leads us to you."

Despite the accusation in her eyes, he knew the truth. "I didn't do it."

"Then prove it. Produce Elspeth. Unharmed."

Didn't Babette understand that he'd like nothing more than for Elspeth to appear? The damned note burned in his pocket. He yanked it free. "I don't know where she is, but she left this." He thrust the scrap at Babette, who snatched it.

Her brow furrowed as she read. "What the hell is this supposed to mean?"

"It means I don't know where she went. I was following her scent trail to this floor when you arrived. I was about to check the kitchen. You know how she is about food."

"She's not there. First place I looked. I checked out most of the first floor of the main house actually and didn't find any sign of her. Her scent just goes cold by the back door."

Now his blood truly ran cold. "Perhaps she had an early errand to run."

"With whose car?"

"She can fly."

A snort spewed from Babette. "She might be crazy, but even she wouldn't take off in broad daylight. Not to mention, I don't smell dragon anywhere. Do you?"

No, he didn't, it was if she'd vanished into thin air. "She can't have disappeared. Have you contacted whoever she reports to?"

"I am who she reports to." Babette slapped a wall with an open palm, the sound sharp. "Enough with the crap. Where is Elsie?"

"I don't know." The simple truth, and said with a sigh because he expected what happened next.

"Then that leads me to the second reason I'm here. Lucifer, Shining One, you are under arrest on suspicion of murder, illegal use of magic against others, kidnapping, and entering the Emerald Sept territory without proper permission or declaration of species and intent."

"You can't be serious." He blinked at her. "I popped out of Hell into the ruins of a castle in the mountains. Report to whom?" His spin straightened. "And as for your murder and kidnapping charges, for the last time, I didn't do it."

"Tell that to the king. Will you come willingly?" It was then that he noted she wore leather gloves, probably to ensure she could handle the dracinore cuffs she removed from her bag.

"You're working with Maedoc."

"I work for my king," she said, dangling them. "These were a gift."

"You do realize you're being manipulated." Luc couldn't have explained how this benefited Maedoc and his brother, but surely they did it for a reason.

She approached him, hypnotically swaying the cuffs by her side.

She was small in size, but he didn't make the mistake of thinking Babette would be easy to evade. Good thing he could use magic. Even if erratically. The dracinore worked strongly in this dimension, just its presence nearby disrupted the flow of magic around him.

He'd have to find another way to beat… He glanced at Babette's sad expression, and he realized she didn't want to do this. Just like he didn't want to fight her.

She only followed orders, orders based on lies.

Someone intentionally made me look guilty.

But who would listen?

In this world, everyone outnumbered him. Only a few people ever chose to listen. One of them stood in front of him, but she was letting duty and love for her friend cloud her reason.

Yet he had to try. "Listen, Babsy," Luc said, adopting the name Elspeth used. "I understand things might look bad right now. But I swear. I did nothing to Elspeth. I haven't hurt anyone."

"I wish I could believe that." Babette shook out her hands, and the fingers turned into dragon paws tipped in sharp claws. Her face took on an alien cast, and her eyes glowed.

Luc waited for the anger to flush him hot and draw out the demon. He didn't have full control of his other side yet. Repressed for his entire life, the ability to change shape was like a muscle atrophied from lack of use.

The rage, which helped his inner beast pulse to the surface, remained dormant.

He looked at Babette. How could he fight her? He meant her no ill will. The idea of hitting her repulsed him. Was this why his father had refused to go to war? Because it involved hurting people that hadn't truly done anything to—

Whack.

Her solid blow to his head caught him by surprise. Because he'd not actually thought she would attack him. His jaw went sideways without his face and snapped.

Ouch.

He shook his head as he staggered. "I didn't do anything—hey." Luc danced out of the way of her slashing claws.

Babette ranted as she attacked. "Do you have any

idea how much it pisses me off to have to do this? I trusted you, dude. Trusted you with my bestie. And I'll tell you, it wasn't easy to call her that. I mean, Deka will always be my main friend, but she's got a man now. And Elsie…well, she's a good sort. Nuts. But I actually like that about her. Plus, she's tough. Which is why you better not have hurt her, asshole!"

Luc found himself in the position of having to defend himself against the blows. He saw a few opportunities to retaliate.

Yet he held back.

He couldn't hit Babette. She wasn't his enemy. She acted right now out of affection. Caring. For Elspeth.

He could understand feeling a little crazy about that because now he was getting worried. Where was his curly-haired bundle of sunshine?

"Last I saw her, she was sleeping beside me. When I awoke, she was gone."

"Likely story. I know you two weren't sleeping together. Elsie's a good girl. Which is fucking rare and beautiful. If you ruined her…" Babette swung the fist with the cuffs. He ducked.

"Last night was the first time."

Babette stopped, bouncing on the balls of her feet to snicker. "First time. That's funny. Guess it's been a while since we could say that."

Given he wasn't about to admit his shame, he turned his head.

"Holy shit." She punched his arm. "Do not tell me you were a virgin. Two fucking virgins. Oh my God. Is that why you killed all those girls? None of them managed to get your gander going? Did you ever think of grabbing men instead?"

He blinked at Babette. "I now see where Elspeth gets some of her logic from. For the last time, I didn't kill anyone. Or kidnap anyone. I need you to concentrate for a minute. Listen to what I have to say. Elspeth is missing."

"Because you hid her?" Babette said on a querying note.

"No! I would kill for Elspeth. Burn the world down to ash if she asked. She is my universe. My everything. The—"

"Dude, I get it." Babette held up a hand. "Let's stop before you have me puking. Let's say I believe you. That you had nothing to do with it. Explain why the evidence leads here."

"What evidence?"

She began to tick off her fingers. "Uber records for two of the victims. Cell phone triangulation for three more. And then there's the fact that a spectral trace done on the most recent body showed it dying in this castle."

"What is a spectral trace?"

"If the brain hasn't decomposed too much, there is a thing we can do. It requires a reputable medium, who doesn't mind getting dirty in a paste made of body parts and spider spit. The medium sticks their hands in it, and they instantly know the exact location of death."

"Do they also see the face of the killer?"

"Actually, they see nothing. Not even the death itself. But don't think that gets you off the hook. One of those murders happened here. In this house."

"According to your magician. Perhaps their spell is flawed because I didn't do it."

Babette chewed her lip. "I want to believe you,

but…let's say I do, who else could it be? Who else lives here?"

"Only Alfred and, well, you've met him."

"I have. He's a snotty sort. Where did you find him?"

"Right in this very castle. He was tending it for his previous master."

"Don't you mean mistress?" Babette tilted her head. "This castle was being used as a B&B by a Mrs. Chesterville. She hasn't been seen in over two months. Not since you took over. Did you get rid of her?"

"Me?" No need to feign shock when it burst out of him in that exclamation. "You cannot blame me for her disappearance. I've been here less than two weeks."

"Impossible. The girls started going missing before that."

"Because I am not responsible. Like I've been saying."

A furrow formed on Babette's brow. "But if you're not to blame, and Elspeth is missing, who took her?"

The cleaning crew? Some unknown agent?

"When was the last time you saw your butler?" Babette asked.

"Alfred?" Surely not.

He took off with long strides toward the area he knew Alfred had taken as his own. As he approached the door off the kitchen that led to Alfred's quarters, he suddenly veered, heading back for the main part of the house.

He noticed Babette frowning from the door. "Where are you going?"

"Nowhere."

"You look like you're confused about where Alfred lives."

"Nonsense. He lives off the kitchen, there." He pointed over his shoulder.

"Then why are you going this way?"

"Because…" He stopped. Why had he turned around?

He peered behind him at Alfred's door, recalling how he'd wanted to go in, but now… Why did he need to go see? How ridiculous to think an old human could have the power to abduct a dragon as capable as Elspeth.

It just wasn't likely.

Which meant it wouldn't hurt to look and see how Alfred lived past that door. He whirled and approached the portal and managed a hand on the knob before he was strongly reminded why he shouldn't enter someone else's private space.

It's rude.

He turned away and noticed Babette close to him, gaping. "Dude, that was freaky cool. My turn. Let's see if the door makes me walk away and look like a zombie."

Luc didn't understand what she meant as she stepped past him, humming, "Gonna make it to the door and open it and look at me reaching and…" She paused and pivoted, her eyes out of focus.

Utterly fascinating. "I never even saw the spell," he mused aloud. However, now that he knew…

Luc took a few deep breaths and placed his hands together to focus. He mumbled words under his breath using the language of magic his mother had taught him, a series of guttural vowels and fluting consonants. The noise fluttered to take shape and then pulsed as he fed power into it.

A blanket of magic, a shimmer in the air, spread in front of him and moved as he took a step toward the door.

Within a pace of it, his shield quivered and appeared as a greenish mist in the air, but it worked. In the sticky web he'd cast, he'd snared the edges of the spell guarding the door.

He blew a few more words into his web, heating them with his breath, fanning them to hotly spread into the shield. It warmed, growing hotter and hotter, binding the other spell in its grasp until *whoosh*. The whole thing ignited, and the magical aftermath drifted like motes of sparkling dust.

"Dude, that was all kinds of cool," Babette breathed in admiration. "No wonder Elsie likes you. You'd be awesome at parties."

The attempt at levity did not quell his sense of urgency as he finally flung open the door leading to Alfred's quarters.

He'd never realized the castle had two wings. The half he'd chosen to live in was vast, impressively appointed, and too much space for Luc.

That space was mirrored in this wing. It turned out that the kitchen door wasn't the only entrance sealed by magic.

He'd never seen it.

The fact that Alfred literally lived like a king in the wing next to him astonished. The farther they penetrated, the more stunned they became. Babette was particularly impressed by the mess.

"Dude, Alfred is a massive hoarder."

"He's a collector, all right," he repeated. Especially of food. Sweets reigned supreme. Rooms filled with boxes of candy. There were also chocolate bars and licorice. Minty peppermints and sour gummies. The goodies, though, were less disturbing than the room with chains dangling from the ceiling and blood on the floor, brown and black stains that obscured a drawing

He still recognized it.

"That's a triangle of power." He pointed.

"What does it do?" Babette skirted the waxed edges of it.

"It's a focus to enhance a spell." At Babette's blank look, he expanded his description. "Magic is like a very fine powder. When gathered together, it's dense, but without something to keep it bound, it falls apart. It's the decay in a spell. Magic users expect it. But sometimes, to conserve magic or keep it from dispersing as quickly during bigger undertakings, a magical triangle is used."

"What you're saying is that this is some kind of demon magic thing?"

"Yes." Luc exited the room with its stink of magic —and death.

"Is that your triangle?"

"No."

"Which means, Alfred's a demon."

"Impossible. He smells human."

"Dude, that is not seriously hard to fake. Follow me."

Luc kept pace with Babette, who took the stairs to the second level with the bedrooms.

"Where are we going?" he asked. "And what did you mean that it wasn't hard to fake? Is it possible to change one's scent that thoroughly?"

"With today's perfume and the science labs to create

them, we can smell like anything we want. Don't your people have a demon recipe to do the same? Some kind of magic spell?"

"I don't know. Maybe. I never had access to all our teachings."

"But you know about some of your history and traditions."

"As much as my mother and the others could teach me before their demise. The rest I learned from reading."

"They brought you books?" Babette flung open doors on the second level as she asked. More spaces crammed with stuff.

"They had no choice if they wanted to learn. The dragon mages, even Voadicia, had difficulty learning our written language. Mother claimed it was because only those of the blood—demon blood," he explained, "could read our words. When Maedoc and Eogan chose to keep me, they didn't do so out of altruism." They'd used Luc, bringing him books with promises of treats if he translated for them.

"Where does Alfred fit into all this?" Babette asked, pulling her head out of a room filled floor to ceiling in teetering piles of jeans.

"I don't know." How did a human get involved in the affairs of demons and dragons?

Babette marched down the carpeted hall, the cushion of the tight weave not allowing for a satisfying stomp. At the end of the corridor, she flung open the wide double doors.

Given Alfred's scent was strongest here, he wondered what they would find in the master suite.

"This is way nicer than what I have," Luc remarked, noticing a level of luxury he didn't enjoy.

A gigantic bed with a plush, burgundy cover and plump pillows. The four-poster held diaphanous scarves, and he had to turn away lest he think of Alfred using them.

He stepped farther into the room and noted Babette lifting a lacy undergarment with the tip of her boot. "These are perfect for the sniffers."

"Are they good at following scent?"

Babette blinked at him then snickered. "Oh, they like to smell stuff, all right. And pay to do it."

Since he didn't understand—and probably didn't want to—he stepped away from the bedroom area and headed toward the bathroom. The place where a person was most likely to have their guard down—and leave a trace.

The huge, marble-covered room held an antiseptic smell.

"It's spotless," Babette remarked from behind him.

A little too clean given the state of the bedroom. Jars were lined up on the vanity.

Babette pulled them forth and lifted the stopper on the first jar. She smelled. "Minty with a hint of bleach. Probably for his teeth." She went to the next. Dabbed her finger in some cream and watched her finger prune. "That is some seriously messed-up, backwards and forwards aging shit." Indeed, making something older rather than younger. Who would do that unless…

"Hey, this cream makes it young again." She held up her finger, now plump and healthy.

"The last one will be scent," he predicted as she yanked on the last stopper.

She leaned down to sniff then turned her head to say. "Human. An old, human male. Not even a whiff of it being fake." Babette straightened. "If Alfred isn't human. Isn't old. Isn't anything at all, then who is he?"

"One of the dragon mages. And he's got Elspeth!"

Chapter Twenty-Two

During the entire conversation over breakfast and the invitation to get in the car, Elspeth knew Alfred was the bad guy. She didn't know why, or how, but the moment she'd noticed him in the kitchen it hit her.

He's the tool of my death.

The perennial double agent. He'd fooled her good. Bamboozled the girl who could see the future. But the good news was, she was finally on to his game. The bad news was, according to her vision, this was where it possibly ended.

At least she'd gotten to enjoy one stupendous day with Luc. It was more wonderful than she could have imagined. She wouldn't be greedy and hope that fate would propel her past this moment.

Why can't I be greedy? She'd waited most of her life to finally meet her mate. Had spent one glorious night in his arms. It wasn't enough.

I want more.

She only had herself to blame. How did she not see Alfred's perfidy?

Because I look for the good, not the bad.

No wonder Mother insisted she needed a keeper. A keeper might have thought to bring an umbrella.

Plop.

A raindrop struck her nose. She blinked open her eyes and discovered herself tied to a stake outdoors.

Not too bad on its own. She'd been tied more than once in her life. At least this time, she wasn't gagged, tied to a cinder block, and dropped in a lake. Good thing she could hold her breath.

More worrisome was the pile of sticks at her feet that appeared to extend around the stake and a few feet from it. A touch disturbing.

Alfred stood in front of her, alongside Maedoc, who rubbed his chin. "Awake already. Stronger than you look. I do so love healthy dragon stock. Hopefully, there's some of that spirit left when we're done with you."

It just lacked ominous music to make his words worse. As it was, Elspeth didn't like the sound of them. Her vision had never revealed if her demise would hurt or not. She just knew death hovered nearby.

"You do realize, once my dragon brethren realize what you're doing, they'll be quite upset. With good reason." Elspeth was a ray of sunshine in their lives. She forced a smile to her lips.

Maedoc smirked. "We already have allies from within the dragon Septs who are fully on board. It would seem their new Golden king has left them unimpressed. He moves too slowly, and he lacks higher aspirations."

"We have the numbers to rule the Septs then the world!" Alfred declared.

"Do you know how villainous it sounds to say you want to rule the world?" Elspeth exercised her eye rolls.

"It's the natural order. We used to be the rulers of this land," Maedoc declared.

"Not in recent times," she argued. No pills made for a grumpy Elspeth.

"Dragonkind hasn't ruled the world since they banished their strongest members."

"You mean the dragon mages?" Elspeth didn't need a vision of the future to see how this was going. "I won't deny the mages got a raw deal. The guilty ones should have been killed." Mercy only went so far. The lives that could have been saved had their ancestors shown a little more balls would have seen Voadicia and the others dead before they'd had a chance to perpetrate their evil.

"But they didn't kill the guilty. They decided to lay the blame on all magic users. Those Goldens and their superiority complex. This was their plan. To send us away so they could rule unfettered. Instead, the humans almost decimated them. They should have kept us around. Now, they'll all pay."

"But we had nothing to do with your sentence. You're killing innocents."

"We were innocent before being imprisoned," Maedoc snapped. "Some of us mere children when we entered the Hell dimension. Punished for something we were never aware of."

"You could have lived in that world peacefully."

"We did that for a while. It got boring, and then we found some books. Magic books." His irises flared red.

"And the rest, as they say, is history." Maedoc spread his hands, a beatific smile on his lips.

"The humans will kill you."

"Have you seen it in a vision?" Alfred fixed her with a stare.

Uh-oh, did they know about her power? "I used logic. The humans outnumber us and aren't about to allow anyone to rule them." Especially not criminals from another dimension.

"All we need are the right steps. The perfect acts to make a play for domination." Alfred gestured to his brother. "Maedoc has a plan to achieve that."

"In order to guide our future, we need to see our future," Maedoc elaborated.

The idea that they might take her power brought a smile. "You want my visions, go ahead and take them. Tell me what to do. They've been nothing but trouble."

Eogan, who looked less and less like Alfred the more he rubbed some lotion into his skin, frowned. "You're lying. No one wants to give power willingly."

"It's been a nightmare. Literally. Do you know how many futures there are? It's exhausting." Elspeth would welcome a quiet mind where she could only guess at the future like everyone else.

"To know is to be all-powerful."

"Except I don't know everything. For example, why pretend to be Luc's butler?"

"Because it amused. We never expected the demon to follow us through the portal, but when we realized he had, we saw an opportunity."

"For what?"

"To lay the blame at his feet. To use him again as

our servant." Eogan shrugged. "He is alone. We planned to make him into the perfect scapegoat."

She frowned. "You were using him."

"We use everything we come in contact with. It's a specialty of ours." With his youth returned, Eogan's smile only enhanced his handsome appearance.

"If you're done bragging about our greatness, let's get started," Maedoc announced. He pulled a pinch of powder from a pouch, tossed it into the air, and blew, chanting a weird string of syllables.

The motes were pulled toward Elspeth and began churning around her. It caused a small breeze to appear, tugging at the loose curls of her hair.

She blew at them to keep them from her face, a little more worried than she wanted to admit by the weird tornado forming with her at its core.

The wind, whistling around, muffled the chanting. The twining speed of it blurred her vision of Maedoc and Eogan, the latter now a young man in his prime.

What her cousins and aunts wouldn't give to get their hands on that cream he used. Pity things appeared dire, and she couldn't see one spit of the future past this moment.

That didn't mean she was giving up.

The spinning winds stole her breath. She clamped her lips and peered around as she wiggled her hands, looking for any slack. Fear didn't quite have her in its grip yet. *Because this isn't how I die.*

The spinning vortex began to pull at her, not just physically but also at a cognitive level. Much like someone yanking taffy, her memories stretched out of her—a long, thick chunk of visions. Dozens of timelines tugged away.

She didn't fight it. She let them go.

Those were the visions that had never come to pass. They took up valuable headspace.

She let the pair grab those memories and more. Let them siphon the millions of things she held inside. With each yank, she felt herself growing lighter.

Faint. She closed her eyes, and her head lolled.

She dropped into a vision.

Luc, looking fierce and lovely. "Elspeth, where are you?"

"Right here, silly," she giggled.

"Are you hurt?"

"Not yet. But I imagine it will hurt when they light the fire."

Grawwrrr. He roared in her vision. She snapped open her eyes and realized she still heard a roar.

In real life.

The taffied memories continued to spool from her, freeing up corners of her mind that she'd lost long ago. The cobwebs were swept. The attic cleaned. She felt great. At peace. Empty. Only her personal life memories were left. As it should be.

But the taffy puller wanted more. The vortex tugged at the core of her, yanked at her true memories kept hidden in a vault.

Um, no thank you. She shoved back at the wind.

It insisted. *Hand over those memories.* Memories that would give them secrets they shouldn't have.

She thickened the shield. *They're mine. Don't touch them.*

He tried, though. Just had to poke. The nerve. And from a banished dragon mage no less.

She dropped the dreamy face. Slammed the door of her mind shut.

Then knew what she had to do.

Get rid of Maedoc and his brother.

They shouldn't be here, feeding on the innocent.

Both should have died a long time ago.

Don't think like that. Happy thoughts.

Happy thoughts were to combat the bad visions.

She had none right now.

Just me, myself, and an ancestry that says you don't fuck with a Yellow dragon.

Bring on the arrogance. As her hands wiggled in the rope, her body swayed slightly side to side, testing the pole. She needed more time. "You are breaking the terms of your banishment."

The whirling wind dropped in time for her to see Eogan sneer. "I'm pretty sure I could argue in a court that we've more than served our sentence."

"How do you figure, given you've committed even more atrocious acts?"

"Says you. There's no one alive to say otherwise." Eogan smirked.

As for Maedoc, he was bent over at the waist, holding his head.

"He doesn't look so good."

"He'll get over it. It will take him time to process the influx of information from your head."

"It might also drive him insane."

"Possibly. I guess we'll see." Eogan smiled, made all the more evil because of his beauty. As Alfred, he was an elderly, distinguished gentleman, propriety personified. Having reverted to a young man, he was now virility on steroids. Handsome, fit, and projecting some hardcore boy-dragon hormones.

If it weren't for her day with Luc, she might have felt a quiver. Now, she just felt anger. Rage that this man who should have died centuries ago was standing between her and her happily ever after.

"Why couldn't you have just lived quietly?" she asked.

"We were quiet. Subtly building power and staying alive for the day we'd return. Now, we want to make some noise."

"You won't get away with this."

"I don't expect to. And might I say how nice it is that you're still coherent and feisty. I really thought that you might be a babbling mess after that spell. It's why I had you put on the pole. But now, I'm thinking maybe we should reconvene elsewhere. With fewer clothes and some chains."

Elspeth fluttered her lashes. "I'd rather die," she said sweetly.

He laughed. "You say that now, but I promise you will beg me for it. Harder. Faster. You'll totally ask for—"

"Death." The word emerged almost like a sibilant hiss despite the lack of an S in it. On its heels, a shadow descended from the sky. Massive, winged, the body thick and muscled, his tattoos darker than before. A bigger version of Luc with horns and cloven hooves, his skin a charcoal gray and leathery.

Her demon.

He came.

She'd not been sure he would, but knew any kind of possible future relied on it.

With his appearance, her magic stirred. Possibilities brewed, but she didn't have time to sift through any visions.

She needed to get off this pole, especially once she

saw Maedoc lift his head, eyes gleaming a pure red, no whites left. His voice, deep and ragged, commanded, "Light the pyre. It will destroy the demon."

Luc roared and dove at the brothers, who split. From overhead, she heard a trill, and she craned to see a silver streak.

"Babsy!" she yelled. "Knock me over, would you?"

The silver body immediately banked and dove for the pole but didn't reach it before the fireball that hit the dry kindling.

Whoosh.

The heat of it singed the air, and Elspeth knew her time was limited. She'd have to move fast.

Babette came in and alit behind her, giving the pole a shove hard enough to make it groan as it cracked.

However, a dagger tossed by Eogan drew a sharp cry before Babette could completely free Elspeth.

He hurt my bestie! The smell of dragon blood was distinct.

The other brother sauntered closer. "If it isn't the Silver Voadicia was fucking." Maedoc smirked. "How's it feel knowing you betrayed your people?"

Babette blarted something rude.

"Go get him, Babsy. I got this."

With a trumpet, Babette flung herself off the pyre, one of her wings sporting streaks of blood and a small tear. But that scratch wasn't the biggest concern of the moment.

The flames licked, and the smoke thickened. Elspeth couldn't waste time. She flung herself left and right. The weakened post snapped and fell over.

It didn't quite free her. She tumbled down the pyre, singing her clothes, ignoring the burns as she rolled clear of the burning pile. She inched up the pole until her arms were freed. It took a bit more wiggling to slide her arms to the front.

Then the gnawing she'd practiced came into play, freeing her wrists. Under a minute. Must have been cheap rope.

She sprang to her feet and ran just as a fireball hit the spot with the remnants of her pole.

"Missed me! Missed me! Now you get to deal with me," she sang, sprinting toward Maedoc, who was probably the more dangerous of the two.

Some might think, *so what if he hummed off-key?* Except she knew he wasn't making music. He was preparing to cast a spell. A big one. Which is why, when she ran past Babette, she grabbed the dracinore dagger protruding from Babsy's wing.

The humming turned into an open-mouthed chant, and she knew she had very little time to stop him. To save Babette.

But her legs just weren't long enough, her pace not fast enough. Good thing she'd practiced knife throwing.

The blade left her palm hilt over tip, spinning in the air, catching fiery glints. She was feeling pretty good about her toss. About to cheer.

Thunk.

The pommel hit Maedoc in the chest, and the knife fell to the ground.

He looked up and smiled. "My turn."

Uh-oh.

Chapter Twenty-Three

Caught dodging spells, Luc only absently noted the bright yellow out of the corner of his eye. Elspeth had drawn on her dragon.

She'd need that extra layer of toughness because the brothers were hard to kill—as he'd learned to his chagrin.

Somehow, Luc had thought that turning into his demon would solve his problem.

Especially given how much it hurt!

Having the skin flayed from your body probably felt like a tickle compared to turning into a massive beast, though. Luc might have screamed in a very unmanly fashion when his rage over Elspeth being taken finally made him snap.

His beast had popped out. Quite literally. Wings and all. The tail had especially stung.

But he couldn't help feeling a sense of pride. He'd done it. Tapped into his demon self. He was strong. Fierce.

I'm coming to save you, Elspeth.

He went to dash out of the house, only to find himself foiled by a pair of towering appendages and a single kitchen door, the combination requiring him to detour out of the kitchen to the front.

Emerging outside, the morning sun caused him to blink, allowing Babette to catch up.

"Where are you going, dude?"

"Elspeth." Her name emerged as a rumbly growl.

"I get you want to save her, but we don't even know where she is."

"I know." His yell for Elspeth had resulted in her answering in his head, but he'd take it. At least it gave him a direction to go in. "We go this way."

"You found her?"

"Bad place." He found himself incapable of speaking more than simple words. The calmness in Elspeth as she accepted her fate had caused a panic in him.

He'd lost so much in his life already. *I can't lose her, too.*

He jumped. And landed. Jumped harder, yet hit the ground rather than soar.

"What are you doing?"

"I am going to get her." He forced the words out as he flapped his wings a few times. He didn't even levitate an inch.

"Try giving it a running start," Babette remarked.

He dashed across the ground, flapping his wide, gray wings and accomplishing nothing but annoyance. He yelled.

Babette yelled back. "That's a boy. Scream. Because that will help Elsie."

He whirled and glared. "I could destroy you."

"Elsie wouldn't like that."

True. "Only if she finds out."

"Listen, dude. I don't like you, you don't like me. That's cool, but we both like Elsie, which means we have to work together."

Which was how he found himself on a parapet about to jump.

Of course, Babette never let him count to three. She shoved. He fell.

Like a rock.

He used magic and managed to keep from becoming a demon pancake.

Once aloft, flying became easier, but he never let go of the magic. Babette streaked silver alongside him. Following the tug on his psyche that told him where to go, he soared through the sky to Elspeth's rescue.

The first glimpse of her tied to a pole, her dress flaring in the wind, a bright red beacon, he lost what control he had left.

He roared.

The perpetrators, those who'd had a hand in taking Elsie, killing his family, and torturing him were both present.

Maedoc and Eogan. The last of the dragon mages.

Kill them, said the spirit of his mother.

Mercy, said his father.

Luc always was his mother's son.

He went after Eogan first since the silly man had chosen to keep his tiny, fleshy body.

"I will rip out your heart," Luc said, alighting on the ground, his hoofs gripping the earth.

Eyes a bright red, a sign he held magic, Eogan raised his head and cackled. "Little demon boy. You should have stayed in the castle. Now, you'll get to watch me eat your girlfriend."

Luc roared as he charged Eogan, who danced out of his way. Luc rushed past and stumbled, completely missing.

"Clumsy demon. I've lived forever compared to you. Do you really think you have the strength and skill to beat me?"

The thread of doubt sought to weave around Luc. He batted it down and stood to face his enemy, chest heaving. "Evil." The only word he could mutter.

"Evil is in the eye of the victim. I see myself more as a conquering hero. I survived. And I will continue to survive because I am not afraid to fight."

"Then fight," Luc growled. He moved in, closed fists swinging.

Eogan evaded, moving with a sinuous grace Luc envied. Then, the dragon mage attacked.

Eogan lashed out at Luc, yet it wasn't a fist that hit him but a punch of air. It flung him back to hit the ground close to the burning pyre.

He rose to his feet and faced Eogan. He studied his opponent. Fit. Human. Overly confident. Probably because he had a sleeve full of spells to lob at Luc.

However, Luc also had magic. Pure demon magic. Whose was stronger?

He began to huff out through his nose, an old technique his mother had taught him for focus. Others stamped their foot. Or snapped fingers. As he huffed, he tugged at the river of magic coursing through this place. This world was so plentiful.

Eogan laughed. "I see what you're doing. Do you really think you can outmatch me?"

"No." But Luc hoped to outsmart him. He didn't attack Eogan. He did nothing overt with his magic. Rather, he sent it down into the ground, sent it deep and imagined, more than felt, the tremor.

Eogan lobbed electrical blue balls at him. "You really should have stayed behind or at least not gotten involved."

"You took Elspeth."

"Which was an error. Our plan called for her to be taken after your arrest by the dragons."

"For crimes *you* committed."

"And framed you for. Damn demons and their murdering ways." Eogan's lips curled. "Once they find her body and your scent all over her, they'll make the only assumption."

"That you'd look better without your head." Luc flicked his hand and sent several missiles of pure energy, crackling balls that snapped and sizzled, at Eogan, who ducked them and laughed.

"Is that your best?"

Luc flung a large rock, and as Eogan ducked, Luc said, "No, that was a ploy." The ground underfoot rumbled and then cracked right under Eogan's feet.

His features took on a startled appearance then shock as the ground continued to crumble, forming a large hole. Eogan didn't have a chance to escape.

Throwing himself aloft, Luc hovered over the hole in time to see Eogan bounce off the sides of the chasm, long hidden under the ground, an old volcano mouth grown over, the lava tunnels raging with water. Eogan's limp body hit the torrent rushing through, and Luc saw the bobbing body bang the wall a few times before getting sucked into a tube.

Which left just one more threat.

Hovering mid-air, Luc pivoted to see Maedoc firing bolts of light at the dragonesses. Babette bore several burned streaks while Elspeth dodged each one as if she knew where to expect them.

Did her visions help her? A handy trick if they did.

But she should not have to dodge at all. He drew more magic to him and gathered it until he was full.

He pulled enough that even Maedoc noticed. He turned with wide eyes to exclaim, "What are you doing, you dumb demon?"

Skin sizzling with power, his veins coursing with energy, he smiled. "This is for my mother, asshole."

Then, Luc clapped his hands, sending out a wave of pure, menacing magic and obliterated the dragon mage.

Chapter Twenty-Four

Luc didn't wake up for two days. Two days of chaos where Babette and Elspeth had to explain to their Golden king what had happened. Stand witness as Joanna, who'd betrayed her Sept, received her punishment, and Elspeth's mother appeared, thinking she was going to drag her daughter home.

"I'm not going with you," Elspeth told her mother while standing outside Luc's bedroom door.

"You can't stay here. With him. The king hasn't made a decision about him yet."

"Either he kills Luc, or he doesn't. Either way, I'm not leaving."

"He's a demon. Not a dragon."

"I know."

"He might try and use you."

To which Elspeth replied, "He's my anchor in the storm."

At that, her mother's lips pressed together, and she nodded. "Are you certain this is the future path you wish to take?"

More than anything. If he woke up. Elspeth wasn't sure yet when or if that would happen. She'd gone back on her meds, not easily she might add. The temptation to know what the future held was a powerful thing.

However, it also took some of the surprise out of it.

Elspeth might have to numb her emotions about a lot of things, but when it came to Luc, she wanted to feel everything. Even the fear that he might not wake up.

She kept close, snuggling him, talking to him, even bathing his still body.

On the third morning, as she returned from the kitchen, she squeaked as she was grabbed and hugged. The biggest and bestest hug of her life.

"Luc!" she exclaimed.

"The one and only."

"I was so worried. The Silver physician couldn't figure out what was wrong with you."

"Magic overload. I funneled too much, too quickly, and burned out. Did it work?"

"Maedoc is no more."

"And Eogan?"

"We've not yet found his body, but given the violence of those tunnels and the current, it seems unlikely he survived."

"If he did, then he will require lots of time to heal."

"How do you feel?" she asked as he turned her in his arms.

His steady, blue gaze met hers, and his lip curled at the corner. "Well-rested. And you?"

"Happy now that you're awake."

"I wouldn't leave you now that I've found you."

"Promise."

"My life for yours." He lifted her off the floor and

squeezed her tightly, swinging her around, cracking something in her spine.

Her entire body loosened, and she laughed. "The future is going to be epic."

"Did you see it?"

"Nope. I don't have to. I just know it." She kissed him, a soft embrace of hello.

He took her greeting and turned it into a more carnal one, the kind with tongue.

He frog-marched her back toward the bed, but rather than lay her on it, he turned her so that her buttocks pressed into his groin. He murmured against her ear.

"I heard you while I was recuperating."

"Oh. What did I say?"

"More like what you promised to do." His hands were deft as they stripped her. When he had her naked, he pushed her toward the mattress.

She crawled slowly onto it, presenting her posterior, warming his groin.

"Are you just going to look?" she said coyly.

His hand rubbed over her butt, and he said softly, "Are you sure I'm what you want?"

"Very sure."

"I heard your mother while I slept. Your king hasn't made a final decision."

"I don't care. You are my mate."

"Are we? Mated, that is?" He drew nearer, his hand pushing down his boxers, revealing himself, hard and long and ready.

"In my heart, we always were."

"We should make it official."

"How does a demon mate?" she asked.

"I'll show you."

He crawled onto the bed behind her, and she remained on her hands and knees.

He ran his hand down the length of her spine, right by the cleft of her ass and then dipping lower.

She caught her breath. He touched her again.

Her head dropped as he slid a finger into her. Then two.

The honey of her sex eased his way and slicked his wet digit over her clit.

Her face ducked low enough that her cheek pressed against the sheet. Her fingers fisted the bed linens while her lush ass presented itself to him.

Luc positioned himself behind her, the tip of him probing. He placed a hand on her shoulder, the other on her hip as he pushed himself into her. Then he slammed his cock into her welcoming sheath, and she felt the wet glove of her sex tightening around him.

"Yes," she hissed as he pounded into her willing flesh.

He woke her body, and she loved that he wasn't gentle about it. His passion ran as hotly as hers. As he kept thrusting into her, the tension in her tightened.

He murmured encouragement. "That's it, my beautiful mate. Sing for me."

Sing? More like high-pitched cries and ragged breaths as she neared climax.

"Are you ready?" he panted.

"Yes."

At the moment of ejaculation, he whispered it, that most powerful word of power. A word a demon could only use once in their lifetime. It was binding.

A tie between them.

Pure love in its most beautiful form.

When the spell finished twining, she gasped his name. "Lucifer. I claim you, too." Then she turned her head and bit the hand on her shoulder.

He yelled. She laughed.

But it was done. A dragon and a demon, mated. The world trembled. However, she didn't feel it, cuddled in his arms. Her haven from the storms of the future.

Epilogue

Months later…
    Elspeth swung high overhead, the specially installed aerie garden in the multi-story gallery well worth the price. It made his dragon mate happy.

If she were happy, then Luc was happy. A simple way to live life. And make no mistake, he was living. Happily, too.

Elspeth balanced on the swinging seat, her lithe yellow body sinuous and graceful, the wings behind her a gossamer ray of sunshine.

Beautiful. To think he'd heard some muttering that her bright yellow was too glaring. Too bold.

Luc called it just right.

Everything about Elspeth was perfect.

With her, he was learning all about this world. Discovering happiness along the way—which, it turned out, wasn't just in bed. He'd recently discovered licorice. A delicacy he'd decided to hoard in honor of his dragon mate. Although, when Babette asked about their truckloads of deliveries of the stuff, he'd claimed it was for Elspeth's secret stash.

Elspeth didn't mind the little lies. According to his mate, she tucked those special things they did together in that mental vault of hers. It became her sanctuary, the place they visited together when one of her dark vision spells hit because he'd encouraged her to wean off the pills. She should never have to hide what she was, just learn to control it.

Especially since more than ever, they needed to see what was coming. They'd weathered one storm, but Luc feared they sat in the eye of another with the worst yet to come.

The future loomed cloudy and uncertain. The winds of fate were whipping. The cracks of possibility all around them.

Soon, they'd see what fork the world entered.

Humanity might be fucked. Maybe even dragons and demons, too, but until then, he'd live and love.

DEEP IN A DESERT, the sand trembled. Slid. Slid downward even more as if a stopper had been pulled, and it all ran out.

From within the funnel appeared four shapes atop steeds made of bone. The riders wore armor that absorbed all light. They trotted up the side of that funnel of sand as if gravity did not apply to them; the heavy plods of the hooves making steady progress up the slope.

Across the world, Elspeth trembled against her

husband, and suddenly, the many chattering versions of the future went quiet and still.

THE END...YOU tell me. Should we do one more?

FOR MORE EVE Langlais books and news, visit EveLanglais.com

Made in the USA
Columbia, SC
30 October 2018